COLLECTED SHORTS

By

JOHN W. WARNOCK

ISBN: 978-1-60643-755-1

DEDICATED TO:

Marianne, Chris and Clay,
but especially Marianne,
my muse whether she likes it or not.

Thanks To:

My family, who put up with a lot.

Bruce, David, Lori, Mark, Roger, Ruth, Steve
and all the other members of Thursday night's
Writer's Exchange group.

My cousin Marilyn Moore
and friend Doris Guerrant
for their sharp eyes and wise counsel.

Also by
John W. Warnock:

Reunion

Tom Skolstad is a pawn in a high-stakes game of espionage and murder. The problem is: he has no idea he is playing. He has been compromised by North Korean Agents using psychotropic drugs. Can he escape the playing field before he is killed? A fast-paced thriller with lots of twists and turns set in Washington, D.C.

ISBN: 978-1-43825-636-8

Psychic

Joe Fitzsimmons hasn't been the same since the accident. The visions and blackouts are ruining his life. Things only get more complicated when he falls in love with his neurologist. He can see things in her past that affect her present, their future and put his own life in danger.

ISBN: 978-1-43825-733-4

www.JohnWarnock.info

Collected Shorts

John W. Warnock

CARLTON's WOODS

To see Jerome "Speedy" Huffington come racing out of Carlton's Woods was not a sight for the weak at heart. Had Jerome been a girl, he would have been described as full-figured. He was obese to the point of needing a bra. The sight of him in the high school locker room after gym was enough for most of the boys to involuntarily turn their heads if caught looking. Of course, it was his mother, and only his mother, who called him Jerome. To any new acquaintance, particularly peers, "Jerome" was quickly corrected to "Jerry." The "Speedy" part was part middle name, part characterization. It was Jerome Speedwell

Huffington, III for the record. But to anyone who witnessed his normal slow lumber, "Speedy" was pure irony, which is Ralph Taylor thought it odd to see him come running out of the woods.

Every student in New Caanan knew its history. Carlton's Woods was named after Colonel Jamison Carlton, a rather sorry military figure who led a band of colonists to their doom in those very woods at the hands of Indians, during King Phillip's War. Colonel Carlton was someone whose ego or self-image was not diminished by his own lack of skill or ability. He was convinced of his prowess at military strategy and, as a matter of course, led a band of twenty or so colonists into an ambush.

Conditions of war were more harsh then, and seeing there was no Geneva convention (the Narragansett being unfamiliar with Switzerland or its continent), no prisoners were taken. Scalps were freely removed, however, whether their owners were dead or merely soon-to-be. Carlton, they say, was not so fortunate to fall immediately. His pleas to be killed went on for some hours, heard by the handful who escaped into the woods.

It was said Carlton's white mane was highly prized and appreciated in value during the period it was traded inside the tribe. At any rate, the dead were left where they fell, and it was six months later before conditions changed enough to allow a small, cautious party to return and inter the bones, scattered by animals. Supposedly, his scalp was recovered at the end of the war and quietly buried in the woods with him.

More than a century and a half would pass before what would become the state would finally erect a memorial to the fallen.

The actual grave site had long been neglected and forgotten in collective memory. A cast-iron historical marker between the highway and the woods would be the only gravestone these sad pioneers would see. It was overly generous to Colonel Carlton's memory to be sure, and completely ignored the territorial encroachments and settler's raids that preceded the incident, but then the plaque was limited in size, labor being so expensive.

These woods, with their sorry history and rocky ground, were left undeveloped for all these centuries while the town, its factories, houses and schools, even its churches and cemeteries developed all around it. These woods dominated, literally as well as figuratively, as did the Huffingtons. It was small wonder that the area developed a lore over the years. Sightings and tales of wandering spirits grew and became embellished over the centuries, largely by adolescent males, as one would expect. Naturally, Colonel Carlton himself figured prominently. It became a male rite of passage to spend one night in the woods. Local scout troops made it a point to have an annual camporee there. An evening of history and ghost stories around the campfire was usually capped by an accomplice in the woods, acting the part of the tortured Colonel, pleading to be killed.

These were, of course, evening activities, which is why it was so odd to see Speedy Huffington racing at full throttle towards the highway in the bright sun of midday. It was odd and comical to see Speedy do anything fast, and Ralph Taylor, one of his classmates, who was thumbing a ride into New Caanan, would have laughed except for what happened next. Speedy, yelling something incoherent, came bounding out of the woods towards Ralph.

Ralph just stood there, awed by the vision of anything so large moving so fast. Ralph was, in fact, considering and rejecting numerous clever options of what to say to Speedy when he finally got close enough. But Ralph grew further distracted at Speedy's approach when Jerry's color and expression became clearer. Speedy was normally pink (and often sweaty), though perhaps this was just Ralph seeing Speedy exert himself in gym. Here Speedy was neither. He looked white and clammy, which was odd for someone of such bulk undergoing such exercise. Ralph frowned as Speedy approached, slowed and then collapsed. Dumbstruck for a second, Ralph walked, and then ran over. Speedy's color was shifting from white to blue gray. He lay on his side, his face in the gravel, his eyes open and pained. Ralph knelt down. "Jerry, what's going— "

"Don't let them get me!" Jerome suddenly lurched up and grabbed Ralph by the shirt. Ralph, surprised by the move, involuntarily pulled back, losing several buttons. Jerome held on. "Don't let them…" His eyes never changed, although Ralph felt his grip loosen. Jerome thudded onto the gravel, facing the woods. Ralph stared a moment, dumbstruck, then realizing his situation, he jumped up to flag a passing motorist.

The rest of that afternoon, mercifully enough, passed in chaos for Ralph: the motorist, the police, the ambulance, the hospital. It really didn't strike him until the newspaper article the following day. Jerome "Speedy" Speedwell Huffington, III was dead and he was the last person to see him alive. It was not unnatural for someone in Jerome's condition to die of heart failure, the doctor at the hospital had said. College athletes had collapsed on the basketball court for goodness sake! At the viewing two days later, Ralph would be lucky

Jerome's parents were too much in shock to pursue what had happened.

Jerome's mother was unapproachable at the funeral home. She was supported by what Ralph assumed to be a sister at either side, all three puffy-eyed and weeping uncontrollably. Mr. Huffington — *the second?* Ralph wondered — stood quietly to the side, remarkably composed under the circumstances. Both of Jerome's parents were stocky, as were Jerome's brother and two sisters sobbing off in the corner. *The Huffingtons are an easy family to spot in a crowd,* Ralph noted.

It was with considerable awkwardness, that Ralph entered the parlor, not having been to a funeral since his grandmother's, and then only to the church and graveside service. He hovered by the doorway, transfixed by the crepe-lined gray steel object at the end of the room. It was something he didn't care to see, and yet was driven by curiosity to approach. A man in a dark suit touched him lightly on the shoulder, directing Ralph closer to the guest of honor.

"You look like a strapping young man. I'll bet you were one of Jerome's friends," the man said with hushed assurance. It was Nolan Gartner, the son of Gartner and Son Funeral Home. Old man Gartner was long gone, and it was his father who took the livery stable from horses to corpses. Gartner and Son was one of the few ongoing concerns in East Hampton, the shoe business having moved to the Far East over a decade ago. "It's such a shame isn't it? So young. Looks like he's sleeping doesn't he?" Gartner smiled.

"Uh, yes." *Sleeping in a box, in his suit, in make-up,* Ralph thought, but Ralph was much closer to the body than he wanted to be, and quite distracted. It gave Ralph the appearance of quiet control, however.

"I hate to ask," Gartner continued, "but we're looking for pall bearers. Would you mind?"

Ralph nodded absently. You couldn't tell by looking at Jerry that anything out of the ordinary had happened. *What had happened?* A small voice seemed to pop out of nowhere. He abruptly turned to Gartner the son, now an old man himself. "What does a pall—"

"It's very simple really," Gartner pointed to a line of wooden folding chairs, a green cloth cozy covering each back. "Just sit in that row of chairs at the service tomorrow. I'll show you what to do when the time comes."

The man must have said that a thousand times. And with that, Ralph Taylor, the last person to see Jerome Speedwell Huffington, III alive became one of the last people to handle his corpse. Mr. Gartner smiled, placed a hand approvingly on Ralph's shoulder and, seeing what might have been one of Jerry's male cousins, moved off to enlist another recruit.

Ralph slept fitfully that night, perhaps disturbed at the sight of the body at the funeral home. He slept well enough the night before, but that must have been the shock of the events of the day. It was like he kept dreaming and waking, but couldn't remember what the dreams were about. He moved about the house in a sort of a daze, his parents deferring to him. He showered, and put on his suit, shivering at the thought of Jerry in a suit, too. He declined his dad's offer to drive. Ralph had been driving barely six months, and this was an opportunity to go somewhere alone. He swung by Ed

Nelson's house. Ed, too, had been enlisted by the efficient Mr. Gartner.

"Got the old man's wheels. Wanna cruise the strip mall afterwards?" Ed greeted Ralph as he got in the car. "It's Saturday. Shame to waste the suits."

Ralph shrugged. He was driving his dad's Buick, another reason to chauffeur himself. Other than family trips, this was his one chance to pilot the land-yacht. Electric everything and buttons galore! At four years old, it was still better than driving his mom's beat up Taurus wagon. They drove on towards Gartner's.

"So, ya got to see old Speedy croak," Ed ventured. Ralph shot him a look. It was piercing observations like this that made Ed a lifelong friend. "Cool. What was it like? Did he drool or crap in his pants?"

Ralph found Ed's innocent curiosity endearing. Again, Ralph shrugged. He hadn't noticed. He really must have been out of it that day. "I don't think so," was finally all he could manage. Luckily, they were already in the parking lot of the funeral home. The boys climbed out of the car and wandered in. Gartner was happy to see them and Ralph was happy for an occasion not to talk.

The funeral went very much like an abbreviated church service. Ralph's mind wandered off frequently. Fortunately, he wasn't tempted to laugh as he had feared. The pall bearers were seated in the front and to the side. It was a good spot from which to see the show. At the appropriate moment, Gartner motioned for them to rise. The family and friends filed past Jerome for one last time, the family hanging off to the side. The crowd having passed, Gartner closed the lid of the casket with quiet efficiency and nodded to the eight young men. Ralph, Ed, and six others divided into two teams of four and moved to either side of the casket. The job was really easy as the coffin was on a rolling stand. *Afraid of accidents or lawsuits,* Ralph thought.

They rolled the featured attraction up the center aisle and out the door in the hallway which was now open. People were milling nervously around the doorway and in the parking lot. The pall bearers reached the back of the hearse, which was open. Nolan Gartner thought of everything. There wasn't even a door sill to stop them. They were on blacktop and under cover in moments. The only lifting was to raise the casket onto the rollers on the back of the hearse. Gartner was there to guide them. The pall bearers stepped back and to the side to watch the casket eerily glide inside by itself. The funeral director quickly folded the stand, closed the rear door and motioned for the family to get into the limo.

Ralph, Ed, and the others all filed into their cars. Ralph was surprised to find a flag marked "funeral" on top of his car. *Gartner really has it down to a science,* he thought. He started the car and got into line behind the others, conscious for the first time of the age of his dad's Buick.

"Why was he running out of the woods?" Ed wondered aloud.

"Huh?" Ralph cocked his head, and then turned back to watching the car ahead.

"Was there something following him?" Ed continued.

Ralph had to think. *No, there was nothing.* It was odd. There was no one that he could remember.

"Maybe he stumbled into a hornet's nest," Ralph finally volunteered. It was a lie and he knew it. The procession was making nice progress towards the cemetery. It was amazing how well the long line of cars moved.

"So where were the hornets?" Ed wanted to know. Ralph turned into the cemetery and followed the line to a newer section of graves.

"Beats me," he said as he turned off the engine. Ralph and Ed proceeded to the hearse where the others waited. Here the job would be more difficult. The ground would be uneven and there would be no cart. Still, Ralph was surprised the coffin wasn't heavier. *The difference eight makes,* he supposed.

They walked towards a blue canopy Gartner and Son graced the flaps in weathered white letters. A row of the same folding chairs sat facing a complicated chrome lowering mechanism. IT was tubular steel frame with heavy canvas straps stretched across the grave. The grave itself was hidden by a metal burial vault, also supported by heavy canvas straps. Every space it seemed had a floral arrangement, and even the dirt to fill the grave was covered with a sheet of green artificial turf. Ralph and the others filed around the canopy and turned before heading in. They lowered the casket onto the straps, Gartner guiding them every step of the way. The canvas gave a ratcheting groan. Ralph and Ed stepped back with the rest of the pall bearers as the family filed in, took their seats, and the graveside service began.

Like the service at the funeral home, it was hard for Ralph to focus. From where he stood, he had a view of Carlton's woods in the distance. This being a newer section of the cemetery, it had pushed towards the woods before stopping. None of the angel's head stones of colonial times stood here. Nor were there the tall stone pillars of the civil war era either. In fact, there were few stones at all, only bronze and granite plaques at ground level. *Better for mowing*, Ralph supposed.

Ralph stared alternately at the coffin, the minister, and the ground, his hands crossed at the wrists. He shivered. Autumn was just coming in. Leaves were beginning to turn and there was movement in the woods. Yes, movement. And why not? Deer roamed freely there. *Would deer come so close to the clearing?* Ralph caught the movement in the corner of his eye and turned. Too late. It was gone, whatever it was. *Must have been a deer.* Ralph's attention returned to the service.

Amen!" The minister closed, and then announced the location of the luncheon.

Ralph looked up, surprised. He had been somewhere else. Mourners and family slowly drifted from the grave. A few of Ralph's peers lingered to see the lowering mechanism work. Ralph had no desire to stay. He and Ed made their way back to the car after exchanging a few acknowledgments with friends. Ralph was grateful no one questioned his part in the affair.

"So he came running out of the woods," Ed quietly observed. Ralph nodded. "But there was no one behind him?"

"But he kept saying something," Ralph's eyebrows met over his nose as he strained to remember. "He kept saying, 'Don't let them get me.' I don't know."

"Who?" Ed straightened. "Was anybody there? They didn't come out of the woods?"

"I guess not." Ralph and the Buick were both on autopilot.

"Hey, that's my driveway!" Ed was practically thrown through the window as Ralph turned sharply.

"Sorry," Ralph apologized. "I must be somewhere else." He wanted to be alone, but Ed wasn't ready to leave. They sat in his driveway.

"So Speedy thought they were out to get him. How come nobody said anything about this?"

"I guess I forgot." Ralph explained, embarrassed by his absent-mindedness. He had been more affected by this than he realized. "Anyway, it's not like somebody shot him. He died of natural causes — of a heart attack, for Christ's sake."

"Right. Hey, let's go see where it happened." Ed was intrigued by the idea of playing junior detective.

"No, I really should go," Ralph offered, but he was at a loss for a good excuse.

"Come on," Ed pleaded. "I want to see." Ralph shook his head slowly. "You're scared, aren't you?"

Whatever else might be said of Ed Nelson, he was a great manipulator. Ralph found himself uneasily driving to the highway by Carlton's Woods. Ralph blames his current situation on fitful sleep and maybe shock. He woke several times each of the past two nights. That wasn't doing much for his concentration.

"It was an accident—a heart attack. No mystery there." His unease grew. "What are you looking for anyway?"

"Colonel Carlton's ghost," Ed answered with a wicked smile.

"Well, when you find him he's all yours." Ralph pulled the car over to the side of the highway. He and Ed crossed the road, dodging the cars that sped by. "I think it happened around in here." Ralph grew concerned that others returning from the funeral would be driving past the sight. The last thing he wanted was to be seen here.

"Not much to see." Ed focused on the ground, searching. The gravel didn't lend itself to tire tracks or footprints. The Emergency Medical Service people left little behind either, most of what they took being biohazardous.

"See, let's go." Ralph started for the car. His discomfort began to swell, filling his chest and catching his breath. He had no idea why, and it bothered the hell out of him.

Ed bent down. "So, did old Speedy bust his buttons?" He came back with two small white ones in the palm of his hand.

"Those are mine," Ralph said, remembering. "He must have pulled them off my shirt." Ralph took them from Ed. "You really need to have more respect for the dead." He kept glancing towards the woods, looking for something.

"Hey, what's this?" Ed bent down and picked up what looked like a piece of fur. "Some Rabbit must need a toupee." Ed rolled a patch of white fur in his hand. He stroked the long white hairs. It was torn and fragile. "It must have been here a year."

"Probably road kill. Let's go." Again, Ralph started for the car.

"We gotta check out the woods." Ed would not be dissuaded. He carelessly dropped the fur piece on the ground and headed towards the trees. Ralph stooped and picked it up. It looked really old and disgusting. He dropped it and ran to catch up with Ed.

"I really should be going home." Ralph met up with Ed at the edge of the woods.

"Come on. Where's your sense of adventure?" Ed marched on, his eyes focused on the ground.

"Back at the car." Ralph swallowed hard, pausing at the edge of the trees. He had a knot growing inside. Seeing Ed fade into the trees, Ralph took a breath and plunged in. The forest closed in around him like the cold, chilling water of a frozen lake.

CAT'S EYE

(A Tail in the First Purr-son)

W hat a strange pride of animals I live with.

They call themselves humans. They are too large to be feline and are laughably shy of fur. To make up for this, they stitch mats of woven fibers together and wear them. They place great emphasis on this and change these mats frequently. If I had as little fur as these creatures, I suppose I would covet these mats, too. They cover their hind paws quite a lot, too, sometimes with mats, sometimes with the toughened skins of other animals. They can be quite pitiful at times.

Other than their cubs, which come one at a time and not in litters, they tend to walk exclusively on their hind legs. Even the newborns are several times my size, so as a species they are quite imposing. I suppose this explains the concern with their rear paws. Going about in this strange way, they lack the speed and pouncing ability to be good hunters. I have never seen one stalk or kill anything until yesterday.

As in any pride, the female is dominant. She tells the two cubs what to do and tolerates the male being around — a mistake I would not allow. They seem to mate for life, or at least until a more interesting choice comes along. The entire pride must hunt, because they all go out nearly every day. The cubs climb into something very large that takes them away in the morning and returns them in the afternoon. It smells bad and makes a great noise. The female climbs into something smaller that goes away in the morning after the cubs leave. It brings her back in the early evening. It doesn't make quite as much noise or smell as much as the thing that takes the cubs away. The male used to leave to hunt like the rest, but he stopped doing so quite some time ago. It seems to be a point of friction between the male and female. They snarl at each other more often since he stopped hunting.

I can't see how they catch anything. They are awake during the day when most prey sleeps, and sleep during the night when the best animals are out. Every so many days, the female comes in with great quantities of food. I would love to know where she hunts, because it is enough food to last a week. I shouldn't be surprised at the female's success. She is the only one with claws. They are long and dark and don't retract.

The female takes great care to package the food she catches so it does not spoil. She stores it carefully in one spot in their den. I have rarely seen the male bring any prey to the den, except little containers of water he drinks out of. At that, the water is quite bad — bitter and foamy. To see the way it affects the male, I would never want to touch it.

I should take a moment to describe their den. As they are a large species, their dens are enormous as well. They are filled with things to sit and lie and sharpen one's claws upon. I have never seen the female sharpen her claws and yet they are quite formidable-looking. The den stays comfortable year-round. It stays warm when the weather turns cold, and cool when the weather turns hot. The only drawback is that they keep all openings closed. You have to be very tall to get in or out of their den. I constantly have to ask them for assistance. This is one thing the male is good for as he is around all of the time.

They also seem to have lots places in their den to do things. They have places to eat, places to sleep, places to purr and snarl, and places just for grooming. For a creature with little or no fur, they spend a great deal of time nearly every day tending their fur (or lack thereof). The cubs take the least time and require prodding. The female takes the most — about twice as long as the male. And for all the time they take grooming, I have never once seen them lick themselves or each other. Still, each grooming place has a large container of water on the floor. They seem to change it on a regular basis during the day. Thank goodness, or I would go thirsty from that pathetic water dish they leave me!

Lately, I have been watching the female stalk the male. She waits until the cubs go off hunting, then follows him around the den. They snarl and growl at each other. I think the male is afraid of the female's claws. He always backs off and closes himself up in some part of the den. She gets frustrated and goes off hunting. More recently, she took to pursuing him silently. She watches him and goes through his things when he is not looking. I can't imagine what she hoped to find, but it seemed she was tracking him.

I should mention these creatures are not purely carnivores or herbivores. They seem to be omnivores and eat things you or I would find disgusting. So many plants! And things not unlike the dry food they bring for me, only they eat it in the mornings in some kind of milk. I know it doesn't come from the female. She is incapable of such copious amounts. I can't imagine what creature might produce it, but it must be a large one.

The female takes great pride in certain plants that grow outside their den. They have a sickly sweet smell that attracts stinging insects and the small buzzing flying birds, but otherwise seem completely inedible. Sometimes, the female brings the plants into the den and arranges them in the eating place. There they sit uneaten until they wilt and she throws them out onto a pile of rotting plants, which she grinds up and feeds to the living ones. A very peculiar cycle, but it gives her great pleasure. The male and cubs seem to take little notice at all of this behavior.

Besides formidable claws, the female can grasp things with the pads of her forepaws. In fact, all their species can. I suppose this compensates for their poor pouncing ability. There was a time when the little ones showed great fascination with my tail. I had to move very quickly and often hide to stay out of their reach. It must have been envy, because they have none of their own, you know. How pathetic!

They pick up strange objects with their paws and manipulate them all the time. The kits constantly scatter objects from their sleeping places on the floor of the den. This aggravates the female, but not as much as when the male scatters food. The female herself seems to focus on the eating place. A large object there spouts fire from the top and can get very hot inside. The female often takes perfectly good meat, adds things to it, and puts it over fire in a heavy object with a handle until the meat is ruined.

Anyway, the young had gone hunting for the day and the male was preoccupied when the female snuck up on him. She swung the heavy object she uses to ruin meat and hit him on the head. He fell to the floor and she struck him again and again. I was very surprised she didn't use her claws, but he was larger and more powerful. Still, he had no claws to speak of.

She waited the longest time to make sure he wasn't moving. He was dripping blood on the floor. I sniffed it and licked some, but the female chased me off. It had the same salty taste as the small animals that inhabit the ground outside of the den. I thought she didn't share her prey, which is why she waited for the cubs to leave. But then she did the strangest thing. She rolled the male up in a large woven mat and dragged him outside the den. There she took a large stick and made a hole where she put him into the ground under the pile of rotting plants.

All that trouble to kill such a large animal and then not eat it! But I suppose she might feel some sentiment towards him, or perhaps, like a dog, she buried him waiting for his carcass to season. Still, I could have eaten for a month on what she planted. She worked very hard to remove any trace of the male's blood from the den, then went out hunting herself. The cubs returned later, surprised to find the male was gone. They mewed and mewed. The female returned at her usual time and acted surprised herself. These creatures have a very complex structure of growls and purrs. I think sometimes they must be communicating, but they can't be that intelligent to judge by all the peculiar things they do.

She spent the evening preparing food and comforting the cubs. They went to their sleeping places and seemed to have forgotten all about the male. An odd way to prepare for a new mate, I must say. Still, good riddance! He brought in no food — not even a mouse.

CLIVE'S GUARDIAN

Thomas Doc" Jenkins awoke with a start.

The Vikings were pounding the Packers on the TV in the corner, but that wasn't what jarred him to consciousness. Someone was banging on his front door. "Keep your shirt on!" He grumbled. As Doc pulled the heavy front door open, the vacuum pulled the storm door tight. A large panicky-looking man stood there, his balding head fringed with thinning red hair and a beard. It was Doc's brother-in-law Clive Perske. "Criminy!" Doc groaned.

"You gotta help me, Doc." Clive rattled the locked storm door. Clive's dog Belle, an English setter, barked nonstop from the cab of his pickup.

"All right. This had better be good," Doc warned. "Even Clara knows to leave me alone when the Packers and Vikings play."

"I'll meet you in the exam-room." Clive rushed back to his pickup.

Doc assumed Clive was getting his dog and took one last longing glance at the Packers game as he headed down the hallway to his office. He was semi-retired and small animals were no longer part of his veterinary practice. He was content to travel farm to farm for livestock and let the new clinic that opened up the road have the poodles and parakeets. Doc unlocked the bolt to the main door of the clinic and waited. The TV in the living room played the sound of roaring crowds. *Clive has been to the exam room before,* Doc thought to himself and he rushed back in time to see Rod Walker climb off Mike Bennett, the Vikings' running back. Doc's pleasure was short lived as he heard the clinic door open. "Be right there," he called. He lingered long enough to see the score flash on the screen, then went back to his clinic as the commercials began.

"What's wrong with Belle, now?" Doc stepped down into the clinic and down the back hall to the first exam room. He stopped, shocked by what he saw.

A man wrapped in a tarp lay on his side on the exam table. As exam tables go, it was adequate for a German Shepherd and could barely handle a Great Dane. The man's bare legs dangled over the edge. Had he not been so shocked at the sight, Doc might have wondered why the man wasn't wearing pants when it was the middle of January. His face poked through the filthy oilcloth. It was a young, fine-featured face, topped with wavy blond hair.

"What the heck is this?" Doc turned angrily to his brother-in-law. "The emergency room is over in Pikeville."

"I shot him."

"You what?"

"I was duck hunting at Ryerson's pond. A beautiful Canada goose flew down and wham!"

"You're as blind as a bat and you shot some poor angler when it hasn't been duck hunting season for months. You shouldn't even be driving, let alone handling a shotgun!" Luckily the man was unconscious. Doc's blood was beginning to boil. "And now you want me to become your accomplice. If you weren't my brother-in-law, I'd turn you in myself."

"It's more than you think, Doc." Clive began to stammer. "Y-you see, this isn't what it looks like-"

"It looks like my sister was a fool to marry you. I'm sorry she's gone and not you. I'm going back to my game. You and your victim had better be at the emergency room in Pikeville by the next commercial or I'm calling the police."

Doc stormed back out to his living room, leaving a protesting Clive and his victim. Clive's dog Belle barked in the distance.

"I guess you don't know how people really feel until there's a crisis." Clive muttered as he walked over to the figure in the tarp and gently lifted him. He was smaller than average and unusually light. "I guess it's the emergency room after all." Clive struggled with the office door, but finally got it open. A large white feather fluttered to the floor and spun briefly in the breeze before the door closed. It was splattered with blood.

"Shut up, Belle." Clive snapped at the barking dog. He was about to put the man back into the bed of his truck.

"I'll ride in the cab this time, thank you." The voice was strong and authoritative for someone with a fresh gunshot wound. Clive was startled, but managed not to drop his victim.

"You're alive." Clive managed. "Thank God."

"I'll be happy to convey the message." The man may have been recovering, but he was still cross. "Belle!" He called in the same authoritative voice. The dog lapsed immediately into silence. He closed his eyes.

Clive had to wrestle, but managed to get the truck door open without dropping his charge. He slid the figure in as gently as he could while Belle nervously whimpered. Clive almost closed the door when, remembering, he slid the seat belt across his passenger and clicked it.

"I'm not going anywhere." His eyes were still closed. The tarp had dropped down slightly, revealing curly blond hair that covered the tops of his ears.

"It's just that I could get a ticket." Clive got in his side and snapped his seat belt on.

"We wouldn't want that."

"I'm terribly sorry." Clive started his truck. "I thought you were a goose." Clive's passenger gave him a pathetic look as the pickup pulled out.

"I don't agree with a lot of what your brother-in-law said, but having your eyes checked wouldn't be such a bad idea." He shifted, and the tarp fell off of his shoulders revealing a pair of large white wings folded behind him. The top of the left one was bloody and had obviously been shot. Belle grew agitated again. The winged passenger extended a bare arm out of the tarp and patted the dog's head. "There, girl," he comforted. "Everything's going to be fine." She quieted and lay her head in his lap, looking up at him.

"I guess we'd better get you to the emergency room." Clive winced, looking at the bloody wing.

"Let's go home."

"But Doc said-"

"Doc has no memory that we were there. I took care of that." He closed his eyes and smiled.

Things grew quiet. Finally Clive asked, "Are you an angel?"

"A tutelary angel, to be exact."

"Tutelary?"

"A guardian." He smiled. "Your guardian, no less."

"Oh, shoot!" Clive gave the angel a quick glance. "Sorry. Just my luck to wing my own guardian angel."

"It's equally my fault for leaving you alone and taking physical form. Letting my guard down like that," he shrugged, "I really was a goose! There was an old paddle on the pond I wanted to practice water rescue with, and I thought you'd be all right on your own." The angel shook his head. "You and a loaded shotgun. What was I thinking?"

"I'm very sorry."

"Don't mention it."

Clive studied the wing. "Does it hurt?" He started to cross over into the oncoming lane and was about to hit a tractor.

"Watch it!" The angel shouted. "I'm not in a position to guard you at the moment."

"Sorry, uh-"

"Esamel."

"Excuse me?"

"You were about to ask my name. Well, it's Esamel."

"Esamel," Clive repeated. "I kinda thought it might be Michael or Gabriel."

"Those are archangels." Esamel eyed Clive and shook his head. "They don't waste their time on mere mortals."

"Oh." There was a hint of disappointment in Clive's voice. "My name is-"

"Clive. Yes, I know. I've known your name since before you were born."

Clive stayed silent for a while, then repeated his question. "Does it hurt?"

The angel glanced at his wing then at Clive. "Not in the way it would for you. We're shielded from strong feelings. Pretty immune to hot and cold, too."

"Won't you need to see a doctor?"

"We self-heal." The angel smiled. "I should be fine in the morning. Until then," he sighed, "I'm stuck in physical form."

Clive turned the old Ford 150 past a mailbox down a long dirt driveway. They stopped in front of a small, dormered house that hadn't seen paint in years. "We're here." He offered.

"I know." Esamel quietly answered.

Clive walked around to the passenger side and opened the door. Esamel had managed to release the seat belt. "I can help you a little." He put his right arm around Clive's shoulder. "Careful with the wing, please."

"Sure." Clive reached under and behind the angel and gently lifted him out. Belle got up, but hesitated as Clive turned to go to the house. "C'mon, Belle." She jumped down and Clive kicked the truck's door shut. A rusty "clunk" confirmed it had closed.

Clive carefully climbed the porch steps. He hadn't shoveled them, and they were now packed with ice. He pulled the storm door open with his foot — another repair project not done. Clive was able to turn the knob and nudge the front door open. The living room was a mess of clutter and dirty dishes. Belle came in and started cleaning the plate of stew Clive had eaten that morning. Kicking the front door shut, Clive took a long, hard look at the stairwell in the corner. The angel was beginning to get heavy.

"The downstairs bedroom will do just fine," Esamel suggested.

Clive was momentarily surprised that his guest should know so much about him, then realized the angel would know everything. "It hasn't been aired out."

"The south windows get sun most of the morning this time of year. It will do just fine." Esamel eyed his host. "Besides, you sleep upstairs."

Clive hesitated, then carried his guest through the obstacle course of a living room, through the dining room and to a closed door. Clive struggled to turn the knob. The paneled door swung open to old, familiar smells. He hesitated, then carried the angel across the threshold. Three lace-curtained windows let light from the declining winter sun into the room. Long shadows crawled among the photos and bottles atop an old mirrored dresser. Clive sat Esamel on the foot of the bed. The angel steadied himself against one of the tall wooden posts.

"I'll pull the covers down." Clive drew a tasseled knit spread off of the pillows and turned back a thick blanket and fine sheets. He helped Esamel get under the sheets and sat him up in front of freshly plumped pillows. "Are you hungry?" Clive finally asked. "Can I get you anything?"

"Hmmm." The angel thought for a while. "Something chocolate?"

"I've got some hot cocoa mix in the kitchen."

"That will do just fine."

Clive left, and the angel heard him fill a kettle and put it on the stove. Esamel studied the room. Dusty as it was, it had feminine traits. The walls were decorated with a flowered wallpaper. The photos on the dresser were too numerous and sentimental for Clive. The angel studied the view of fallow fields that lay outside the windows. A few minutes later, Clive returned with a steaming mug of cocoa.

"It's a little hot, I'm afraid."

"We'll see." The angel took a loud slurp. "Ummm." The smell drew Belle into the room. She wagged her tail in anticipation. "No marshmallows?" Esamel asked.

"Sorry."

"Just kidding." Esamel drank as Clive nervously watched. "This was your room," the angel finally observed.

"Yes."

"She died here." He glanced at Clive.

"Yes."

"I'm sorry." Esamel returned to the cocoa.

Clive stood watching. "Can I ask you something?"

"Shoot." The angel winked at him and smiled.

"Where was Emily's guardian angel when she died? And for that matter, where were you when I broke my arm sledding on Peterson's hill?"

"A difficult question," the angel took a sip of the cocoa, "deserves more than a simple answer." He indicated the foot of the bed to Clive. "Have a seat."

Hesitantly, Clive sat as the angel pulled up his legs to make room. Excited, Belle jumped on the bed, too. "Belle!" Clive scolded.

"She's fine." Clive grimaced as the angel let her taste his cocoa, then continued drinking it himself. "My job is more complex than just keeping you from harm because of your job."

"My job?"

"Everyone is here for a reason. Sometimes, it is to invent or create something. Occasionally, it is to shape history. For most people, it is simply to raise the next generation to adulthood. And everyone is here to learn something. If nothing else, then something about themselves." He shared another taste with Belle. "Some people would do well simply to learn how obnoxious they were in life." He looked pointedly at Clive. "Admit it. There are people who drive you crazy after five minutes. Can you imagine spending an eternity with them?"

"No," Clive acknowledged. "But what about-"

"Your arm?"

"Yes."

"Sometimes, you have to come to harm to learn something or change history." The angel shrugged. "You were a pretty good athlete before the accident, right?"

"Yes."

"Threw a pretty mean curve ball?"

"That's right."

"And that spring you learned it was gone."

"I got cut from the softball team. They set it wrong."

"So they did. And looking for something to excel in, you let Tommy Elgin talk you into joining the chess club."

"I did."

"Where you met one Emily Jenkins." The angel smiled as a look of realization came over Clive. "I rest my case."

Clive thought for a long time, then turned to Esamel. "Why did she die?"

"Well, that is a little simpler to explain." The angel studied Clive. "I can move from this plane of existence to the next rather easily, when I'm not wounded." He glanced over his shoulder at his wing. "You are rooted here. For you, the only way out is death. Age and disease are His way of telling you to let go and get ready." Esamel glanced around the room. "The next realm is really much better than this. Still, you don't know this." He toasted Clive with the mug of cocoa. "And true, we don't have things like this in heaven. I can see where people hang on for dear life, so to speak." He looked at Clive, who was studying the floor with a frown. "I know," the angel grew quiet, "you thought you'd grow old together."

"It isn't fair."

"And if you know that, you've learned something yourself."

"So, what do I have to learn before I graduate?"

"Ha," Esamel smiled. "I can't give away the answers to the final exam. That would be cheating." He studied Clive. "And that's the other challenging aspect of my job: not getting involved — not affecting the outcome God has ordained."

"Oh." Disappointed, Clive rose and took the mug from Esamel. Belle jumped down. "Can I get you another?"

"No." The angel smiled. "I'll sleep now. Everything will be fine in the morning. You'll see." He turned and lay on his right side, his back and wings to Clive. The wound didn't look as serious as Clive first recalled seeing it.

"Good night." Clive stood at the doorway and gestured for Belle to follow him. "I'll see you in the morning." The angel grunted in reply as Clive quietly closed the door. "Pretty interesting day, eh Belle?" Clive set the mug on the kitchen table, turned off the lights and made his way upstairs to bed.

Clive woke to sunlight streaming in the upstairs window. Belle lay quietly at the foot of the bed. Her head rose as he stirred. "What time is it?" he asked the dog. He pulled on a terry cloth robe that hung on the back of the door and returned to search under the bed with his feet for slippers.

"C'mon, Belle." He said to the dog, who jumped to the floor. "You need to go out, and I need coffee." Belle barked once and raced him down the stairs.

As Clive passed through the living room and dining room to the kitchen, he found Belle scratching at the bedroom door. "What is it, girl?" He turned the knob and the dog rushed in. She spun, barking and sniffing the air. "What is it, Belle? Mice? Squirrels?" Clive looked around. Belle whined and grew still. "See? Nothing." He held the door as the dog dragged her tail into the kitchen.

"I don't know why I'm climbing the stairs to go to bed every night." Clive spoke to no one in particular. "This room seems just fine to me." He was about to go to the kitchen when something caught his eye. Picking a large white feather off the bed, he asked, "How did this get here?" He shrugged and went to let the dog out.

.

THE REVEREND

IS OUT

"F irst Reformed of Snow-

"Oh, Ruth, it's you!

"No, you're not disturbing anything. I'm just stuffing church newsletters. The Reverend is out making home calls. It's like death here. You know nothing ever happens in Snow.

"I know. I couldn't believe it either! That red! She looked like a fire engine. I could understand if it was Pentecost Sunday, but she's the minister's wife for goodness sake! She should know better.

"Uh, huh.

"You'd think he would talk to her, wouldn't you? Why was she trying to draw attention to herself?

"You think? Wait. Let me put you on hold...

"First Reformed of Snow.

"No, Reverend Pflinghoffer isn't in right now. Can I take a message?

"I see. I have no idea when he'll be back. Sometime before noon, I suspect.

"Yes. You're welcome. I'll be sure and let him know.

"Ruth. Are you still there?

"Good.

"No, it sounded like an attorney.

"He wouldn't say. I'11 bet old man Huddleston left the church something in his will. Anyway, he said the Reverend was to call him immediately upon his return.

"Uh, huh.

36

"It would be nice, wouldn't it? Maybe we could get new cushions for the pews. The Reverend's sermons have rambled lately, haven't they? I hope they don't blow it on new hymnals.

"Uh huh. Sure.

"Now look at this. I've got an address label here: Tom and Bev Metterman. Remember them?

"She was the petite blonde the Reverend took a real shine to. Tom was older. Real quiet. They dropped out last year around Lent. Used to be regular churchgoers. Now they've fallen off the face of the earth.

"I know. And after all the time Reverend Pflinghoffer spent calling on them at home. My Carl saw her at the Safeway about a few months ago.

"He did. He comes home and says to me, "Dolores, there's something odd going on there. It looked to me like Beverly was getting over a shiner!"

"Yes! Of course, the Reverend never discusses what goes on at these visits, but it must be spousal abuse, don't you think?

"Uh, huh. Yes, it's a shame. But what can you do? Just a minute, Ruth...

"First Reformed of Snow-

"Oh, hi, Ellis—

"No, the Reverend is out right now. He's making home visits-

"I have no idea where-

"No, I don't know when, eith—

"Nice talking to you, too, Ellis!

"Still there, Ruth?

"It was Ellis Denninger. I don't know what's got into him. He's gotten so short-tempered lately. Really!

"If his wife wasn't the organist...

"She's a sweetie, isn't she?

"The Reverend's been working a lot with her lately. He thinks she has real potential. They're here until all hours of the night. Of course, how she could get anyplace from this dull, little burg...

"Well, Ruth, it's true! The Founder's Day parade is the one big event we've got, and that's only a band, two floats, a fire engine and a tractor. The band peels off the front and races to the back to make the parade seem longer.

"No, I didn't know he was musical either, but they must teach that in theological seminary. Don't you think?

"Anyway, he's said several times that she has a real gift.

"Oh, Ruth, that's nasty. But it wouldn't surprise me. Now that you mention it, there is less gray than I remember. He could be using something.

"He's definitely lost weight. If my Carl weren't the jealous type…

"I think he looks marvelous. He's really taking care of himself. Not like his wife.

"I'm not sure. She seems to get mousier every week. I wonder if she's, well, depressed, maybe.

"Stress? In Snow? Ruth, be real! How could there be- Hold on, Ruth.

"First Reformed of—

"Hello, Esther! We were just talking about-

"No, he's out. I have no idea where, but Ellis called looking for him, too.

"Yes, I was definitely going to let him know Ellis was looking for him. What is this all-

"Don't get hysterical, Esther. It's at the top of my list-

"I'll be sure and let him know. Couldn't you tell me-

"Nice talking to you, too, Esther!

"Ruth, you there?

"It must be contagious. That was Esther Denninger and in a real snit, too. She was as short with me as Ellis was.

"She wanted me to be sure to let the Reverend know that Ellis was looking for him and that he and Mrs. Pflinghoffer have talked, whatever that means. Honestly, I think I know how to deliver a message after all these years.

"She didn't say and he didn't, either. I guess the Reverend knows what this is all about. It's a mystery to me.

"Well, he is very discreet. I never hear what goes on with the parishioners. I'm sure he doesn't tell his wife, either. He's very good that way. Just a second.

"First Reformed of Snow.

"Yes?

"Oh, yes. You called earlier. Well, he's still not in.

"Uh, huh. Yes, I'm pretty sure he'd be back by eleven.

"Oh. Well, I could sign for it.

"I see. Why don't you deliver it to his home? His wife-

"Oh.

"Well, it all seems odd to me.

"Yes, I'm sure that would be fine. Good bye.

"Ruth, you there?

40

"She's definitely going crackers.

"Who?! The Reverend's wife. That was the attorney again.

"Yes, the one who called earlier. He says he has to deliver something to the Reverend and only to the Reverend.

"That's what I said. Why not let his wife sign for it? But he said it's from Mrs. Pflinghoffer. Don't that beat all? She'll talk to Ellis Denninger, but not to her own husband! How sad.

"Poor man. Who knows the cross he has to bear at home? It's worse than any of us thought.

"I better make sure these newsletters get out. It sounds like it's going to be a bear of a day!

"Well, by Snow standards, anyway. If we had a traffic light, it would only be a blinker. It took six years just to get a four-way stop.

"Ruth, you're terrible! I just meant- Hold on.

"First Reformed of Snow.

"Oh. Hi, Tom.

"No, I haven't seen Ellis, but he's called. So has his wife.

"It sounds like he could show up here anytime. Both he and his wife were looking for the Reverend.

"Tom, what is this—

"Oh.

"All right. I'll be sure and have him call you when he does.

"You take care, Tom. Good-bye.

"Ruth? Another one. Must be a full moon.

"Tom Crenshaw this time. At least he wasn't looking for the Reverend.

"Ellis Denninger. You know Ellis puts in some hours at the rod and gun club when things are slow at the garage? I guess he was cleaning and oiling Bill Thompson's prize skeet rifle.

"Yes. Been in Bill's family for years. Silver inlays on the stock? That's the one. His pride and joy.

"Anyway, Bill shows up this morning looking for it, and it's nowhere to be found. That Ellis! It's no wonder he can barely hold a steady job.

"Tom is making lame excuses and Bill is hopping mad. This should make for an exciting day in this one-horse town.

"Well, Carl wants to go to Lowell for the tractor pull, but just once I'd like to see Saugatuck. They say it's lovely.

"I know. That's a man for you!

"Hold on, Ruth. The Reverend just drove into the parking lot. He looks very rushed.

"I shouldn't wonder. Maybe he can explain all of this.

42

"I've got to go, Ruth. Ellis just pulled up. If you thought the Reverend was in a hurry...

"Hmm. Looks like he wants to show the Reverend Bill's skeet gun.

"I didn't know he was interested in skeet shooting either.

"Now Ellis is showing him how it loads and aims.

"Look at that! They're both excited and hollering. Men! They're just little boys at heart.

"Hmm? I don't know. They've both run off. I can't see them in the parking lot anymore. I hope he's not going to fool around all morning. I've got—

"You heard that, too, Ruth? I'll bet it's Norbert Grubb. He-

"There it goes again. You'd think he'd spend a dollar to keep up his tractor from backfiring all the time.

"Ruth, I'll call you later. Maybe with some gossip to liven up this dead little town.

"Take care, Ruth. Bye."

5
LITTLE BOY BOO

The old white Chrysler climbed the grassy trail.

It was too steep and narrow to call a road. Its endpoint, a lonely cemetery, was used too rarely to qualify the road for state maintenance. It looked like someone spilled gravel among the grass. The car threaded the course of trees and underbrush, weaving dangerously close to the edge several times before coming to a stop in a small clearing.

"We're here, Dad." The driver cut the engine and glanced at the front seat passenger.

"Um?" The old man turned as if startled. Despite the warm May weather, his snow white hair was topped by a blue golf hat. "That trip up still bothers you?"

"I guess I'll never get used to it." Paul felt the sweat on his forehead.

"In time, you will." Grinning, the old man looked over his shoulder into the rear of the car. "Well, look who's here!" A small figure sat quietly behind the driver. "Hello, Boo."

"We're here, Beau." Paul glanced toward the back seat.

"You know your aunt and grandmother refused to ride up this hill," the old man recalled. "They used to get out and walk. Remember, Paul? You weren't much older than Beau here."

"I remember, Dad. I'm surprised the corpse didn't get out and walk, too." Paul checked the rearview. "How are you doing back there?"

"You OK back there?" The old man turned to the rear seat of the car.

"Just fine Grampa," a small voice responded. "Are we there?"

"We're here." The old man winked. "Let's have a look."

He opened his door, swung his feet onto the ground and struggled to plant his sassafras cane between them. The little boy in the back seat jumped out, leaving the rear door open. The driver got out, closing little boy's door before seeing to the old man.

"Need some help, Dad?" He extended a hand as the elderly gentleman rocked forward and back.

"Thanks, Pauly. I got it." He made it up on the third try. Leaning on the cane for a moment to steady himself, the old man surveyed with dim eyes the remote cemetery. Ancient grave stones, some no more than rocks, stood in even rows. Most of the graves, marked by deep depressions, were remnants of the days of wooden coffins with no burial vaults. Many headstones lay on the ground, toppled by frost or vandalism. Beau happily chattered away in the distance.

"We do this every Memorial Day like clockwork," Paul shook his head. "It's like we were never here at all. We're still—"

"Give it a rest, Pauly. Why can't you be happy like Boo over there?"

"He's loud enough to wake the dead," Paul complained.

"I wouldn't worry about it, Son." The old man looked on in amusement. "He's just lonely."

Frowning, Paul surveyed the scene. "There's not a soul up here."

"A desolate spot like this? Small wonder," his father replied. A mourning dove cooed in a distant tree. "Will you look at that!" Something caught the elder's clouded eyes.

Fresh clay covered a new grave near where they stood. Its only decoration was a metal marker bearing the name of the funeral home. The young man moved over to read it.

"David Kinner, it says." Paul looked around, then brushed some spattered dirt off of it. "Died in early March. What's he doing up here, I wonder?"

"Probably a charity case." The old man shook his head. "This is a poor state, but the Kinners were dirt-poor even by Kentucky standards. There hasn't been a burial here in decades." He shuffled over to study the grave for himself.

"Only cost to be planted here is the gas getting up the hill." He turned to his son. "I taught David's father back in '33. Used to bring Saltines for lunch. That was all they could afford." A raucous noise caught his attention. He turned to its source. "Boo! Behave yourself. Show some respect, or you'll wake up these dead people." The noise stopped.

"Dad!" Paul scolded. "Really." He called to his son, "Don't get too close to the edge, Beau. I don't want you falling down the side of the hill. And stay out of the poison ivy!" He turned back to his father. "Anyway, what's with this 'Boo' stuff? His name is Beau."

"I know his name." The old man smiled, not taking his eyes off the boy.

The cemetery had no fence, and needed none. Other than the gently sloping hilltop and the access drive, its sides were steep and dangerous. From where they stood, the narrow clearing, no more than six graves wide, gradually climbed for a hundred feet. The grass was kept low more by the shade from the canopy of trees overhead than by any human intervention.

"Let's get to it." The old man began walking up the slope. He stopped and stared at his grandson frolicking among the dead. The grandfather squinted. It looked as is Beau was chasing something around a large oak tree.

Paul went back to the car and unlocked the trunk. He pulled out battery-powered grass clippers and a pair of green metal cones. Same as the ones from last year, each had a spike at the tip and held an arrangement of plastic flowers set in green Styrofoam. The Wal-Mart price stickers were still attached to each arrangement. He debated whether or not to remove them, then decided their recipients wouldn't care. He walked midway up the slope where his father stood in front of a pair of moss-encrusted headstones.

"Gets worse every year." The old man scraped at the growths on the marble with a small pocket knife.

"Dad," Paul shook his head, "you're not going to make much of a dent with that."

"I know, Son." He sighed and stood, folding the blade and returning the knife to his pocket. "Maybe next year we'll bring some bleach and a wire brush." He stepped back, reverently studying the stone. A breeze swept the scent of pines across the graveyard.

Paul lay the two cones on the ground and started the trimmer. He worked his way around the base of each stone. What little he trimmed was more weeds than grass. Finally, he stood, small beads of sweat gathering at his temples.

"That should last us for another year." Paul wiped his forehead with his hand and stood next to his father. "Beau, come here!" He called to the little boy who was busy playing tag in and around the headstones.

The towheaded five-year-old went for the grass clippers in his father's hand. "We want to cut the grass."

"No, Beau." His father pulled back. "You're not old enough."

"Why not?" Beau stamped his foot on the ground.

Paul knelt next to his son, trying to distract him. "Beau, look at that!" He pointed to the headstone. "Do you know what that says?"

"No."

"It says, 'Jefferson Beauregard DuPuis, 1859 - 1943.'"

The boy stood back, wide-eyed. "That's _my_ name," he whispered.

"And that's where we'll leave you if you don't behave." His grandfather touched the boy's nose for emphasis.

"Dad!"

"Just funnin' with him." The old man tousled the boy's hair and winked. "The dead stay dead. Don't they, Boo?"

Paul shot his father a dirty look. "You aren't the one he'll wake with nightmares." He turned back to Beau. "This was your great-great-grandfather. He was born a hundred and forty years before you were."

"Wow." Beau turn to his dad. "What was he like?"

Paul stood. "I wouldn't know, Beau. He died ten years before I was born."

"Oh." He stared at the granite monument for a moment, then turned to a pair nearby, each with a lamb on top. "Are there lambs buried there?"

The old man laughed. "No, those are children."

"Oh." Beau grew thoughtful. "Who were they?"

"I don't know." Paul shrugged. "Nobody can read the stones anymore. Must be family, though. They're here next to old Beauregard."

"I'm pretty sure one of them was the young son of Beauregard." The old man studied the small stone. "Would have been a year or two older than your grandfather. Died in the scarlet fever epidemic of 1906. The other was his sister. Died the same year."

Paul squatted down to study the stones. "They're unreadable."

"Soft marble." His father shrugged. "Still, it was the best they had in their day."

"I'm gonna catch me a toad, too." Beau's attention was instantly elsewhere.

Paul set the trimmers on the flat top of his great-grandfather's headstone. "Great granddad was born before the Civil War." He turned to his dad. "Did he talk much about it?"

"Not really. He wasn't much of a talker back then. And now..." The old man shook his head. "I never thought to ask him. He was barely five or six when it ended." Paul's father started up the clearing, watching the little boy playing among the few standing headstones. "Our people are all buried out by the church on Little Grassy."

"Why would anyone want to be buried here?" Paul followed his father.

"It's out of the way. Nobody comes up here."

"Except kids making out and smoking pot," Paul snickered.

"Before long, there will be nobody left to tend these graves."

"I'll come."

"You?" The old man snorted. "No offense, Pauly, but you can barely find your ass with both hands, let alone this godforsaken place." He sighed and watched his grandson talking away and hopping over the depressions where the coffins had collapsed. "None of this for me. I made it clear I wanted to be cremated when I go. And definitely no viewing. Just a memorial service."

"You told Mom this?"

"Sure. We talked," the old man sighed. "As much as she would talk about the subject." He turned toward where his grandson was playing. "Boo," he called. "I'm sorry but we have to go!"

"I should have named him something else." Frowning, Paul stared after Beau, who was chattering away.

"Hmm?" The old man turned to his son.

"Mom warned me it was an unlucky name."

"No such thing as luck," the old man scoffed. "Not that kind, anyway. Fate, maybe."

Paul waited a moment before cupping his hands around his mouth. "Beau! Come on, now!" The little boy ran to join his father and grandfather.

"Grampa, we almost caught a frog."

"Did you?" He tousled the boy's hair. "C'mon, we have another cemetery to visit." He walked down toward the car, the young boy speeding ahead. Paul walked alongside.

"Be careful, Dad. Boy, somebody ought to fill in these graves."

"Hmph." Paul's father shook his head. "That'll be the day." He made his way slowly toward the car, pausing for one last look at the two headstones.

They reached the Chrysler. Paul opened the door for his father, who slowly lowered himself onto the seat and swung his feet in.

"Beau! Come on!" Paul called to his son, who was walking intently among the graves with his head lowered. "You can look for frogs back home. Let's go!"

Paul held the passenger door open as the little boy reluctantly got in. "Buckle your seat belt." The old man snickered as Paul closed the door and went around to the driver's side, then got in and sat, almost closing his door.

The old man cleared his throat. "Clippers."

"What?" Paul looked at his father, confused.

"Clippers, Paul." A gnarled thumb pointed toward the headstone where they'd been left.

"Oh." Paul got up and walked over to get them.

The old man and the boy spent a moment in silence.

"Why can't Boo come with us?" The little boy watched a wisp of something swirl atop one of the marble lambs. "His name is Beauregard, too, isn't it? He's family, isn't he? Why can't Boo come, too?"

"This is his place — by his sister there." The old man glanced at the pair of little marble headstones. "This is where he belongs, Beau." He shook a finger at his grandson. "And don't you bother your father with that. He's got enough on his mind."

"Daddy is always sad when he comes here," the little boy observed.

"Well, it's a sad place," the old man shrugged.

Paul got in and turned to his father. "Back to Little Grassy, right?"

Paul's father nodded. "You OK back there?" The old man called over his shoulder.

"Just fine, Grampa." The boy stared out the window at the marble lambs.

"Lead on, son." The old man pointed with his cane.

The Chrysler backed into a clearing, then crept forward down the steep trail.

~ ~ ~

A faint white mountain mist drifted past the two men who were climbing the trail to the cemetery.

"You feel that, John?" The white-haired man with craggy features stopped, listening.

"Feel what?" The man in his mid-twenties stared at his father.

"That mist! You must have seen it at least?" The white-haired man frowned as his son shook his head. "I felt it go right through me," he shivered.

"Come on, Dad." The young man gave his father a pathetic look, knowing the often-told story was coming.

"This is the spot," the father continued, undeterred, "Where years ago, three generations of the DuPuis family: grandfather, father, and son, plunged over the side of this mountain to their deaths."

6

KNOCKING

AROUND THE HOUSE

Oh, the monotony of the days.

There are times I think I'll go mad. The endless repetition. The idle routine. There are breaks, of course. Special occasions. I try not to intrude. Keep to my place and all. There are times I think the family doesn't even know I'm there. I suppose that's the sign of a good domestic. There are times, though, when they do seem to acknowledge my presence (however grudgingly). So few and far between are the moments of recognition.

I've been with this house for what seems like a hundred years. (I've lost all track of time I've been here so long.) Oh, yes, there are calendars, but who has time to look. There's so much to do. And age must finally be getting to me. I can't seem to do as much as I used to. I'm starting to sound like an old person with their complaints. Do forgive me.

I was seventeen when I hired on. My mother died in the great flu epidemic and my father remarried. I never got on with the woman, so it was best I left and found work as soon as I did. I would have left sooner, but father insisted I finish schooling. "You'll not be stupid like them girls at the mill," I can hear him saying. He was from the old country. Did very well for an immigrant. He had connections to the staff here, which is how I got the position.

My, but it was a grand house then. It was fairly new. The yard was well kept then. There was a full-time gardener. Of course, the staff was much larger, too. I'm all that's left now. But then there was a cook and a butler, an upstairs maid as well as a downstairs maid. I did the linens. I wasn't always going to do linens, but I had to start somewhere.

Then there was the Great Crash, and of course one by one the staff went. I tried to pitch in as best I could, but there's only so much one can do. And of course, you can see the result. It's still a grand house. It desperately wants paint, and I think there are termites under the front porch. It's not as clean as we kept it, and the yard... That is what saddens me the most. But still, everyone says what a grand house it is.

There was a garden around back. Not vegetables, mind you, but flowers! Roses, azaleas, mums, lilies — I loved them all. I liked to go into the garden. There were herbs there, too. Right off the kitchen. Mrs. Edmon the cook — she was a widow lady — would send me out for thyme or savory. I'd linger as long as I could, taking in the sights and scents. It was wonderful on a summer's night! Of course, back then the cook house was separate so as not to overheat the main house.

Of course, the garden didn't go right away. It took years of neglect — like the house — for the it to disappear. Well, it hasn't really disappeared. You can see flowers and beds somewhat, but the grass has overtaken all. They just started mowing over the short beds and not replanting the annuals. Now the definition of it is gone. It's just a shadow of its former self, really. The Mrs. keeps talking about reviving it. I hope she does, but there's so much to do.

These folks aren't original to the house. Not at all. As I said, there was the great crash, and then like in so many other situations, there was a decline of the staff, then of the family. The staff whittled down to nearly nothing. The father drank himself into an early grave. The house closed for debt. I wept for weeks to lose them.

The house was really her father's, you know. It was he who financed it with his lumber yard. Built it as a wedding present for them, but kept title to it for himself. Didn't trust the husband I think. Must have known about the drinking. So even after the old man died, the husband couldn't get his hands on it. The house stood deserted, except for myself keeping it up, for I don't know how long. Then she died, too, and the heirs to the trust sold it. Oh, those were dark times, indeed.

This is the sweetest family that owns it now. Mister, Misses, a little boy and girl and one on the way. They are so pleasant to watch. There were other families in between. I've served them all. Watched over the house for them. Good, most of them were. I've hated to see them go, but change is part of life isn't it?

58

Oh, there was a time they considered selling this to an undertaker. Can you imagine this fine old home a funeral parlor? The very thought! Ooh, gives me the chills, it does. The dead coming and going. I did what little I could to dissuade them. In the end, it went to another family. And a good thing, too. The neighborhood is coming back as it turns out. I always knew it would.

People want these grand old houses again. Like the McMartin's across the street. They were fine upstanding people. Every now and then, I see Mrs. McMartin in the window. She seems so lonely. Poor dear. Doesn't get out at all, but then I don't get out much, either.

The house is a much happier place with the family here. The children are so cute. (I look in on them at night.) Not three and five they are. Little Robbie starts school this fall. I shall miss him so will his sister. But she'll have another girl to play with, I think. Don't say anything. It's still a secret. I shouldn't know either, but I have my way about these things.

Anyway, the little ones are so darling. They come looking for me. We play hide and seek. They call me the attic lady. Of course the servant's quarters are in the attic, which is where I live. I do admit to getting on in years. I can't get up and down like I used to. Time catches up with all of us I suppose. There I go complaining again. Dear me!

I sometimes think the mother resents my being here, but I go with the house. She knew that before moving in. Still, I try to keep to my place — not make waves. It is a proper servant that keeps to her place. We don't have many differences, but she always seems to be looking over her shoulder for me. I feel on pins and needles around her. Doesn't want any suggestions does she. So, I make as few as possible.

Still, things are better than they were. Oh, not as good as the old days. Those were grand times, then! How sad they passed. Busy house. Large staff. Always entertaining. The father (he drank himself to death, remember) was always wanting to show off his fine possessions. They were always having some mover or shaker from town society over to dinner. I suppose that's why he took the Great Crash so hard. It was the loss of income and influence that did him in.

Well, who hasn't had their disappointments, I suppose. I shouldn't judge. I'll tell you a secret, but you must swear to keep it. I got myself in trouble as a young girl. I had a dalliance with the chauffeur's son. It was wrong, but I was so young and naive. Of course, we viewed things differently then, and rightly so I suppose. What passes as acceptable behavior these days. Shocking!

In time, I found out I was with child. The chauffeur sent his son away. I know it broke the old man's heart. The shame he must have felt. His son tried to make good on his misdeed, but I refused. In retrospect, I should have accepted. There really was no other option for me. I didn't love him, but what other man would have me with the shame I had brought on myself? I was young and foolish, then.

Henry. Henry his name was. See, it took me a while to remember his name. I am getting on. I can barely see his face. The dark brown eyes with the sandy hair. His heart wasn't in it, either. I knew that. I sensed it. I have a way about these things, you know. He was as relieved to hear "no" as I was to say it. I'm sure his father put him up to it. A proper gentleman, he. Henry was going to be an artist. I never saw him after that — never inquired. I hope he is happy wherever he is.

I worked as long as I could, then went into confinement. We had a more delicate attitude toward those things back then. They are so casual these days. It's shocking! Anyway, I went into confinement and then into labor. (The family was very kind. They could have thrown me out, but chose not to.) But, oh the pain! It was unbearable. A breech birth, the doctor called it. I was in absolute agony. I suppose I deserved it.

It got worse and worse, and then I just crossed into delirium. At last, the pain was gone. I was relaxed and at peace. The shocking thing was that I woke up alone. Not another soul in the room! You would have thought someone would have been there to tend the sick, but I was all alone. And where was the child? Where was my child?

Whatever sympathy or kindness others once showed me absolutely vanished. It was as if I wasn't there. I had expected to be shunned, but not so abruptly or solidly. No one would answer my questions. No one would even look at me. And my child! Lord knows where they took it. Oh, we didn't keep them then. They went to be adopted by respectable folks. People who could give them a home without shame. Someone could have told me whether it was even a boy or girl. I still weep sometimes. It was a hard loss.

Even so, I have the house. I've grown used to the shunning. I keep to my place. The pets don't ignore me. At least the animals and the children acknowledge me. And yet, it is hard — so hard.

But oh, the monotony of the days. The horrible boredom! I wonder sometimes if I'm really here, or just dreaming.

..

7

TRICK OR TREAT

William "Willie" Todd crept along Manly

Manly Street. Despite the gathering dusk, he squinted up toward Pettigru, but saw nothing except other children going house-to-house. He dawdled, a nearly empty pillow case in his hands. His sneakers contrasted with the gray pants and jacket he wore. The jacket from his dad was oversized and reached to his knees. Combined with the flat-topped forage hat and the stripes glued to the sleeves, it made Willie look like an authentic 12-year-old Confederate private. The only other contradiction was the toy M-1 rifle he carried. It had a real wood stock, so it could be forgiven for not being period.

He meandered past LuAnne Albright's house and considered going up and ringing the bell when a noise at the side of her house caught his attention. He started towards a large oak tree. It whistled at him. He cocked his head and moved closer. A red tail poked out the left side of the tree. The tines of a red plastic pitchfork extended out the right.

"Psst!" The overloud whisper was all too familiar to Willie. Tad Hanks poked his head out from behind the tree. "Over here!"

"Tad?"

"Shhh." He warned. "Act casual."

"Wow!" Willie came around the back of the tree. He saw Tad, dressed in red sweatpants and a red hooded sweatshirt. The hood had white foam packing peanuts glued to the temples for horns. A rope painted red and stiffened with a coat hanger hung off his pants for a tail. What really impressed Willie, however, was the mustache and goatee Tad now sported. He moved closer and gently brushed them with his hand. "Are they real?"

"You bet." Tad beamed. "Glued 'em on myself." He groomed the mustache like it was his own. "I couldn't find daddy's spirit gum, so I had to use his embalmer's adhesive. The hair was from a restoration kit of his, too."

"Cool!" Willie was awestruck. "Does it come off?"

"I don't think so. I might have to shave it off."

"Can I watch? I don't know any other twelve-year-old who shaves."

"Maybe." Tad stroked the goatee.   "I'll bet you don't know anyone who's snoozed in a Batesville Da Vinci either."

"You slept in a coffin?"

"A casket." Tad shook his head. "Coffins are archaic, six-sided boxes. They haven't been used in over a century."

"What did it feel like? Did you close the lid?"

"All but a crack. Otherwise it locks and you can't open a casket from the inside."

"I wonder why?" Tad just stared at Willie who went on. "It must be neat living over a funeral home. Why don't they open it for Halloween like they used to?"

"My dad read some article in Casket and Sunnyside saying that it's unprofessional." Tad frowned and poked the tree with his pitchfork. "He is so serious at times."

"What are ya doin' behind LuAnne's tree?" Willie studied Tad. "You ain't hiding from Billy Throckmorton, are ya?"

"Me? No way!" Tad scolded. "I'm not afraid of anything. I was just waiting to make an entrance." He said it like he was trying to convince himself as much as Willie. "C'mon. Let's get going." He started for the sidewalk with Willie following.

"Did you really trip Billy in the lunchroom?"

"He stumbled over his own two clumsy feet," Tad said looking over his shoulder. "I just happened to be there." He didn't sound too convincing on that one either. "It was his bad luck to nail Mrs. Brewster with his Beanie Weenie."

"I heard she was pretty mad."

"That's his problem, too."

"Our problem is going to be staying out of his way tonight. Those eighth graders are mean."

"Big, too."

Willie followed Tad to the front porch of a small colonial. He waited as Tad rang the doorbell.

"Trick or treat!" They both called.

A teenager with a large bowl of candy opened the door. The TV blared in the background. "Great," he muttered as he grabbed a large handful and dropped it into Willie's pillowcase. He did the same for Tad, not making eye contact with either boy.

"Gee, thanks!" They both said as he closed the door without comment.

"Did you see the way he was handing it out?" Willie gushed as they headed for the next house.

"He was trying to run out early." Tad led them up the walk. "I wish all our houses could be like that." He rang the doorbell.

"Don't you two look precious!" A woman with perfect hair opened the door. Her orange sweater was decorated with ghosts and black cats. She offered a silver tray covered with large cellophane-wrapped popcorn balls. "Now just take one."

"Thank you, ma'am." Willie cautiously took one.

"Thank you." Tad forced a smile, but didn't look the woman in the eye.

"You're the Hanks boy, aren't you?"

"Yes ma'am."

"Give my regards to your father. He did such a wonderful job when my mother, Mrs. Shreve, passed away."

"Yes ma'am." Tad smiled. "I'll tell him. Thank you." He turned and led Willie back down the walk. He glanced back to check the door, which had closed. "It took hours to get the old biddy looking halfway decent."

"You got to watch?"

"Nah. My daddy's real funny about that, too, but I heard him complaining to my mother about how difficult she was— a regular raisin."

"'Scuse me?"

"Wrinkled."

"Oh."

66

They continued along Manly street until they got to Pettigru. People at several of the houses complimented Tad on his beard and mustache. He beamed. Willie was about to cross the street to go up the other side of Manly when Tad stopped him.

"Let's check out Broadus Avenue." Tad pointed his pitchfork to their right.

"Broadus?" Willie stared at Tad as if his tail had become real. "There's nothing but big old dead houses on Broadus. Nobody goes there."

"My point exactly. C'mon!" Tad started along Pettigru.

"I don't know." Willie held back. "There had better be some houses with pumpkins."

"There will be." Tad assured him. "Trust me." He started down Pettigru.

Willie looked over his shoulder. He could hear the voices of other trick-or-treaters growing fainter as they walked. He strained, but couldn't see any kids ahead of them. The streetlight above marked an intersection with four dark houses— one on each corner. The back yard of the house next to him was overgrown and unkempt. There were no signs of life, let alone the existence of children. They turned the corner. Darkness the length of the block met them.

"I think we should go back." Willie glanced over his shoulder.

"Don't be a wuss, you-" Tad got cut off.

"Hey!" They were startled by the overloud stage whisper of a high soprano running toward them in a ballerina costume. "Where do you two think you're going?"

"LuAnne," Willie took a step towards her. "Am I glad to see you. Talk some sense into him."

"I got more sense than the two of you put together." Tad glared at Willie and LuAnne. "Willie don't like to take risks."

"It's just as well." LuAnne glanced back to where they had come from. "You'd be taking a risk to go back. I think Billy Throckmorton and Eddie Oliver have been following me."

"Oh, great!" Willie shook his head. "We're stuck."

"We're simply in uncharted territory." Tad shot back.

"We're practically in the business district." LuAnne frowned. "The civic center's just on the other side of those houses."

"I don't care if Candyland is on the other side. It's spooky here," Willie moaned. "I'm going back."

"Say 'hi' to Billy for me." Tad trotted to the front gate of the house on the corner. "You won't have to go far. He's headed this way." Tad rattled the iron gate until it creaked open. It gave Willie and LuAnne time to catch up.

"You're going in there?" Willie stared at the huge dark house. The Mansard roof on the third floor gave it an imposing height. The windows seemed to glower at the trio.

"You'd rather stay here and get pounded?" Tad grabbed Willie's lapel.

"He's not mad at me." LuAnne stood her ground as the gate clanged shut. "Besides, he wouldn't hurt me. He knows my big brother would kill him."

"Why did I have to be an only child?" Willie whined as Tad dragged him towards the door.

"Good." Tad called to LuAnne. "You can tell the police what happened to us if we don't come out."

"Don't come out?" Willie froze at the steps to the large porch.

"C'mon." Tad pushed him between the tall wooden columns. "There's probably nobody at home anyway. We'll just let ourselves in if we have to."

Two ornate oak doors with beveled glass windows faced them. Tad looked around and found a button in a tarnished brass plate on the right frame. He pushed it. A low gong sounded from somewhere deep inside the house. He looked to his right to see a pair of figures rounding the corner. He pushed the button again and was about to try the handle when a strange glow appeared from inside the house. A woman's face outlined with a shock of white hair floated behind it. Both boys froze as the figure approached. The left door swung inward.

"Why, Beauregard, come in. I've been waiting forever for you to return from the war." The voice was hoarse with age. A withered claw grasped Willie's sleeve and pulled weakly.

Turning to see Billy and Ed approach LuAnne, Tad pushed Willie's back until they were both inside. He swung the door closed and quietly threw the bolt.

A gaunt, frail woman in a dark housecoat studied them by the light of her candle. She held it in a quavering hand. The yellow light cast a gloomy flicker on all their faces. "Beau, who did you bring home with you?" She studied Tad carefully.

"Uh, trick or treat, Ma'am." Willie hesitated.

"Beau?" She turned and squinted at Willie.

"No, Ma'am." Willie looked down at her bare feet. "It's Halloween, Ma'am."

"Oh." She heaved a sigh. For a moment, she looked as though she might fade away. "All Hallow's Eve," she said to herself. "Where has the time gone?" She squinted at Willie. "I thought you were my Beau. He's away at the war." The old woman studied him more. "Who are you then?" Willie hesitated.

"Why Robert E. Lee, Ma'am," Tad interjected.

"Of course," she smiled. "One of our boys."

"Yes, Ma'am." Willie confirmed.

She turned to Tad, her head cocked in study. "Horns, a red tail, and a pitchfork." She inventoried him. "You must be..."

"Abraham Lincoln, Ma'am." Tad stepped away from the door. Out of the corner of his eye, he saw LuAnne and two others in front of the house having an animated discussion.

"I suspected as much." She frowned. "Why are you here?"

Tad thought quickly. "I was deposed in a bloodless coup."

"And none too soon," She scolded Tad. "Still, I suppose I can afford to be charitable. Your wife's cousin served ably in Jefferson Davis' cabinet."

"You are too kind, Ma'am." Tad hammed it up. "As part of my repentance, I am forced to go house-to-house one night each year to beg for candy, as is my friend the General here." He nodded towards Willie.

"Oh!" She turned to the young private. "Well, we can't have one of our own going without." She swung around and started up a long hallway. The foyer grew dark as the candle cast deepening shadows on the walls and ceiling of the hall. Tad and Willie glanced at each other, then followed the old woman.

"Don't the lights work?" Willie looked around for a switch.

"The war has brought many hardships as you know, but we bear them with pride." She led them to the kitchen. Tall, glass-front cabinets lined the room. They were all too tall for the woman to reach. The lower cabinets had a linoleum countertop. A large, ancient sink stood by itself on a wall by the back door. The woman set the candle on a table and surveyed the flickering cabinets. "Candy," she mused. "My Beau used to love licorice sticks." Willie made a face at Tad.

"Don't go to any trouble for us, Ma'am." Willie turned to Tad who pointed to his wristwatch and made a stretching sign.

"What southerner wouldn't give their all for Robert E. Lee?" She smiled and looked at an open pantry with bare shelves. "Oh, my." She turned back to the boys. "Would money do? I'm afraid I'm short of sweets."

"Sure!" Tad had a greedy look in his eye.

"Ma'am, you don't need to go to that trouble." Willie ignored the frantic gestures Tad made behind the woman's back. "We'll just go on."

"Oh, but I want to help the cause," she insisted with a twinkle in her eye. "General, would you mind pulling open the drawer in that table? My hands are stiff with arthritis, I'm afraid."

"Sure." Willie faced the table that held the candle. It was barely large enough to seat two people. A lone chair stood next to it. He pushed it to the side to reveal a small drawer. Tugging on the wooden pull, the drawer opened to reveal its contents: a wooden handled fork and a box of kitchen matches. Willie looked at the frail old woman. "There's nothing in here."

Tad shook his head.

"There should be a thousand dollars in there."

"Just a fork and some matches." Willie shrugged.

"Now how can that-" The woman stopped herself and smiled. "General, you aren't looking hard enough."

"The drawer is out as far as it will go."

"Is it?" She grinned. "Reach back in the drawer. Up top, at the center is a small pin you push up on. See?" Willie worked the catch she described, and the drawer came all the way out. "That's it," she instructed, "just set it on the table."

Tad stepped forward, eyes wide. The drawer had a false back and a six-inch deep compartment behind it. "There must be hundreds of bills here!"

"That's right, Mr. Lincoln." She watched as Willie carefully picked one up. He reverently studied the old paper in the dim light. Tad frowned.

"This is a hundred dollar bill!" Willie spoke in a hush.

"My father set these aside in case of hard times. I want you to take all of them."

"Really?" Willie stared at the woman wide-eyed. "I wouldn't want to leave you with nothing."

"I'll get by." She smiled at Willie. "I'll never spend it."

Willie hesitated for a moment, then took a handful of bills and put them in his pillowcase. He looked up at his friend, who stared indifferently at the scene. "Tad?"

"Sure." Tad move to the drawer and picked up a couple of the bills. He studied them before dropping them into his pillowcase.

"Don't let that carpetbagger get it all," the old woman admonished.

"No, Ma'am." Willie gathered up the rest of the money and put it in his pillowcase. He picked up the drawer and slid it back into the table. "Thank you, Ma'am."

"Thanks." Tad echoed.

"I get so few visitors." The old woman picked up the candle. The shadows in the kitchen shifted eerily. "I don't suppose you could stay?" She led them back towards the foyer.

"I wish we could," Willie offered.

Tad looked out the front glass and saw the sidewalk in front deserted. "It's late," he sighed. "I'll bet the other houses are closed."

"You have other houses to visit?" The old woman looked crestfallen.

"I'm afraid so." Willie turned to Tad then back to the woman. "You've been very generous."

"Very," Tad echoed as he quietly drew the bolt and turned the door handle.

"Take care, then." She waved as they stepped on the porch.

"We will," Willie waved back as Tad pulled the door closed. "Thanks again, Ma'am," he called as they turned and went down the steps. "Gee, she was a nice old lady." Willie turned and looked over his shoulder. The foyer of the house was now dark again.

"Yeah, real nice." Tad swung the rusty gate open and they stepped onto the sidewalk. He tried to read his watch from the corner light. "I think it's 9:50. We might get a couple more houses in if we hurry."

"You sound sad." Willie studied his friend. "That old lady just gave us thousands in-"

"Hey Tad, Willie!" LuAnne came running up breathless. "You were in there forever. What happened?"

"Where's Billy and his friend?" Tad looked around.

"He wouldn't stay." LuAnne mused. "Said the house was haunted."

"Yeah?" Willie was practically laughing. "Well, the old lady who lives there just gave us a couple thousand dollars!"

"Really?" LuAnne stopped short.

"In Confederate bills," Tad complained.

"Well, they could still be worth something." Willie countered.

LuAnne seemed lost in thought. "That would make sense, I guess."

"What would?"

LuAnne shivered. "Let's go home." She rounded Pettigru towards Manly.

"What makes sense?" Willie ran to catch her.

"Billy said the ghost haunting that house was a woman waiting for her fiancé to return from the War between the States."

"Her Beau?" Willie asked.

"Yes, her beau." LuAnne walked faster.

"Stop it, you two." Tad lagged behind.

"Well, she did say her father set the money aside," Willie reminded Tad.

"I don't even want to think about it." Tad brushed past them. "I gotta figure out how to get hold of my dad's razor without him finding out."

8 MAMMY'S CHILD

"Leave the window open, Mammy."

The little girl frowned. Her green eyes scanned the old woman, whose own dark eyes gave nothing away.

"Child, you gone catch yo death." The heavyset woman scolded. "It be powerful cold dis evenin." She clucked and turned from the window.

"But the water is hot." The girl rocked in the bathtub, starting a small tidal wave.

"Dat jus yo opinion." Two massive white palms stilled the little girl's shoulders. "Don't be makin' a mess. You been a hanful since you come home from de schoolhouse!"

"Do I hafta wash my hair, Mammy?"

"I don suppose so. You washed it yestiday. You wants I should do yo back?"

"Please, Mammy."

The woman knelt and dipped a loofa in the soapy water and began rubbing the little girl's back in a slow figure-eight motion.

"That feels so good." The child leaned into the strokes.

Mammy shook her kerchief-covered head. "What got yo tail in a knot, I wonder?" After a while, she stopped and rose to get a towel, letting the loofa drop with a splash.

The little girl stood and pulled the plug, grabbing the chain with her toes. "I'm not in a mood!" She disappeared into a large green towel, and stepped onto the floor.

"Careful now, Missy. Dat floor is wet." The woman patted the girl dry as the water gurgled away.

"You're always fussing over me, Mammy." She stamped a small foot. "I'm not going to break."

"That remain to be seen, and not on my watch." The woman straightened her apron and rose to put the towel in a hamper.

"Worrywart," Missy muttered as she went through her bedroom to the closet. She thought she heard a faint "fussbudget" in reply.

"Put on yo nightdress, Missy." The woman swept in and began tidying. "Bedtime be long gone. Yo pappy gone shoot me fo sho!"

"Mammy, why does daddy work so hard?" The child popped out of the closet, twirling a strawberry curl from her forehead.

"Child, dress yoself! You naked as a Jaybird."

"Mammy, you've seen me bare naked before."

"Ah has, but the rest of the world han't. Git away from dat window! Git!" She guided the child back into the closet and clucked to herself, "Lawd, Almighty."

"Why does he work so hard?" The question rang from the closet with more insistence this time.

"He want you to have nice things. He say so lots o' times." The woman lumbered to the bed, pulling down the covers and fluffing the pillow. She moved slowly, her energy nearly exhausted. "A plantation is a mighty big ting to run, Honey Child."

"I wish he was home more." She appeared out of the closet in a long night gown and meandered toward a dressing table. Sitting at a small backless chair, she looked at the woman's reflection in the mirror. "You need a new dress," she observed. "You've worn that for years."

"Child, ah needs lots o' things." The woman put her large hands on the girl's shoulders. They felt dry and smooth. "But ah won't see none o' dose neither." She looked at the girl in the mirror and sighed before picking up a brush. "Missy, ah only gots the power for fifty strokes tonight," she sighed. "You run me ragged, child."

"If I had a brother or sister to play with, you'd get a rest."

"It don't work dat way, Honey." The old woman laughed and began brushing the little girl's hair. "You learn one day. One o' you is all ah kin handle."

"Don't you wish you could have a child?"

The woman chuckled, "You is my child, Baby Lamb."

The little girl frowned, "Mammy, what was my momma like?"

The old woman paused and stared into space trying to jog her memory. The images came slowly from long ago. "Yo mama had the same color hair as you. Only her eyes was blue. An she had a laugh..." The woman touched the side of her face in recollection. "Ah han't knowed her for long. Ah was brought on just afore you was born. Times when you'se her spittin image." She began brushing again.

"Mammy, you're the only friend I got." The little girl searched the woman's face for any sign of concern.

"Lawd, child. You gots lot of friends." The woman continued brushing. "That lil' Hale girl-"

"She is cruel and petty. I hate her. I hope she dies."

"Missy!" The woman drew back. "Dat a mean, un-Christian-like ting to say."

"I don't care. Do you know what she said?" The woman shook her head. "She said her daddy was going to buy you from us. He can't do that can he?"

The woman looked blank and resumed brushing. "Not unless yo daddy want to."

"Has he said anything to you, Mammy?"

"Lawd no, Child. Ah's the last one yo pappy gone talk to 'bout dat." She administered the final strokes. "Dat's all ah kin do fo' tonite. Now, git to bed, Missy." She rubbed the girl's shoulders.

The little girl wandered over to her bed and climbed in. "I wish you could read me a story, Mammy."

"Ah wish ah could, too." She tucked in the covers.

"Next year I'm going to learn how. Don't you ever want to learn?"

"Oh Baby Lamb, it unlawful for us to learn to read."

"That isn't fair."

"Life ain't fair, child." The woman turned her head and lowered the lights. "Now go to sleep."

"I'm going to read for us both someday."

82

"'Nite, Missy." She patted the little girl's head and trudged down the back stairs to the kitchen.

Passing the kitchen table, the woman glanced at an important looking document resting there. If she could have read, she would have easily made out the words "Deed of Sale" at the top. She passed it and the pretty color brochure alongside without notice and moved to a tall alcove in the kitchen wall. Maneuvering into the opening, she lowered the kitchen lights and turned so she was facing the room.

The induction coil automatically cut in, sending steady pulses to her energy circuits. Age was robbing her batteries of the ability to hold a full charge. She cut her visual and audio processing systems off to aid the process. At six in the morning, her "wake-up" program would cycle on. Her day on Rigel 7 would start all over again.

DOG'S BREATH

Oh, boy. Oh, boy. Oh, boy. I've got a new home again. Ryan and Amy and I are staying with Aunt Lydia. Her yard has a fence and I can go wherever I want. No more ropes for me! No sir! Things just keep getting better and better — except for that dumb cat.

Amy said if Ryan got to bring me, she got to bring the cat — stupid fur ball. She does nothing useful at all — just lies there and scratches up the furniture, sleeps, and hisses at me. If it weren't that her poops were so good to eat, I wouldn't have any use for her at all. Do they get mad when I snack from her litter box!

My name is Boy — at least that's what I think it is. It's always "Here, Boy" and "Down, Boy" and "Oh, Boy" wherever I go. I'm kinda new at this puppy stuff. I lived on a farm with my Mama and brothers and sisters, but they all wandered off one day and I had to fend for myself. This puppy work can be hard. I roamed alone for a long time. I was too small to knock over trash cans, so I had nothing to eat for a whole day. Luckily, I came across this place where there was a pile of trash in the back yard. They had old ripe melons lying on top. Normally, I'm a meats and sweets kind of guy, but I was so hungry.

Anyway, I was on top of the heap, working on the melons when this boy shows up. He's got something in his hand he wants me to have: a sausage — a Vienna sausage! Yipes! I'd kill for one of those — only I've still got my milk teeth. He kept it just out of my reach, but I wasn't going to stop until I got it. The next thing I know, I'm in the house, in a collar and on a leash.

Oh, well. The food was pretty good, plus all the extras I could get by begging. Nice soft beds and furniture to sleep on. They do have some dumb rules about when and where to go to the bathroom, though. They can go indoors; the cat goes in a box; but I have to beg to go outside. Geez, did the Mom ever get steamed the first few times I went indoors. Give me a break! Can't a guy even mark his own territory?

They had a big argument when I got there, too. I kept expecting the Dad to show up and chime in, but he never did. I guess that was part of the problem: no dad. The Mom must have felt guilty, because after a little whining, Ryan got to keep me. That's when Amy glommed onto their cat — cranky catnip junky!

Anyway, Ryan and I get along just fine and Amy can keep her dumb old cat — thank you very much — and things are going pretty good. I'm cooped up all day while Ryan and Amy are at school, but Ryan walks me when he gets home, unless he's busy. Then he puts me out in the backyard on a rope. I hate that.

I like food — yes, I do. Don't you know that rope's too short to reach the Mom's compost pile? That's what she calls it. She puts perfectly good food out there and lets it rot. Smells ungodly strong on some days, but I like my food with a little "tang" to it. That's what cheese is all about, isn't it? But there it is — just out of reach.

Did I mention the Mom has a friend? Well, she does. His name is Roger. I think he's pretty cool. Amy and Ryan aren't that wild about him, though. I don't understand why. He's allergic to cats. What more could you ask for in a human?

He comes around a lot. I suspect more so since there is no Dad. Anyway, Roger plays catch with me and has as little to do with the cat as possible. For some reason, Amy and Ryan haven't warmed up to him yet. The Mom more than makes up for it, though. They get together here for lunch when the kids are at school. They shut the bedroom door and make lots of noises. I hate that, because they usually put me out in the yard on the rope, especially when I whine and scratch on the door. They're having fun. Why can't I join in? The Mom even has a pet name for Roger. She calls him her "Accomplice," whatever that means.

Boy, oh boy! The thing I like best is digging in the yard. Oh, sure, chasing cats is a close second, but they won't let me. The cat was here before me — dumb fuzz butt. It just lays around, licking itself. She says she knows something, but it's a secret. Like I care! I won't beg. I won't play her game.

I learned a neat trick the other day. I like to chew on things, especially while I'm working on my milk teeth. I discovered I could chew on the rope. In no time, I was free — not that I would run away. No. It's too nice to do that. Still, I was free to go over to the compost heap. What fun it is to dig there.

I knew I smelled something. The nose knows, as they say. About a foot down into the ground I hit some bones. Lots of maggots and decay, too, but bones, sweet bones! I was in heaven. There were so many, I didn't know where to start. It was a large animal whatever it was.

I started in on one choice bone, when the Mom came out so see what I was up to. She was horrified that I was loose and shrieked for Roger to get dressed and come out. She chased me around the yard, but she wasn't going to get my bone. No sir. I ducked through the hedges and into the neighbor's yard.

Now, I don't know Mrs. Abernathy all that well. The few times I've met her while walking, all she does is rant about her precious yard. I rarely go near the place. Old people do nothing for me. They don't want to play fetch. They rarely walk fast enough or far enough. They never want you in their yard or on their furniture. Crotchety types, mostly.

Anyway, I slid through the bushes into the Abernathy's yard and who should I slam into but the Missus. She screams bloody murder and clutches her chest. Old people are like that, I guess. Then Mr. Abernathy comes around the house with a rake to see what's going on. I just took off and hid under their porch. The old lady kept asking the old man if he saw it, and telling him how horrible it was. I stayed under their house and wasn't coming out.

Soon the Mom and Roger joined the Abernathy's in looking for me. I would have been fine, but that stupid cat came by to see what was going on. She tickled my nose with her tail and I sneezed. Mr. Abernathy must have heard it. He ran into the house and came out with the one thing I am powerless to resist: a sausage. He had me out of the crawl space in no time. Smoky-links — the bastard!

He handed me to the Mom. She seemed a little more upset than usual. All I did was get loose. She just kept looking at Roger in his mis-buttoned shirt and motioning with her head. She kept trying to tell the old lady she was seeing things, but Mrs. Abernathy continued sobbing and clutching her chest. Anyway, Mr. Abernathy went and got his rake and reached under the porch. He pulled out my bone. Mrs. Abernathy shrieked again and the Mom dropped me. I barked and barked, but Mr. Abernathy wasn't going to give it back. Mean old coot!

That's when more neighbors showed up and Roger shouted to everyone that he had nothing to do with it. With what, I wonder? I never found out because that's when the Mom started yelling at him and hitting him. The neighbors had to pull her off him. [Like that's the first time?] With all that distraction, I had my one chance to get back to the compost heap for another bone since Mr. Abernathy had mine.

It was a swell bone, too, and I would have gotten another, but the police came while I was digging and stopped me. I was looking where I found that first one. It was so cool. I must have dug down by the head, because hanging off Mr. Abernathy's rake was a jaw bone complete with gold teeth and silver fillings.

10

PATIENT 3152

"He's at it again, Dr. Chalmers." The massive woman hadn't bothered to knock. She stood, arms crossed, in the doorway waiting for a response. The traditional white nurse's cap looked odd askew such a large head of gray hair.

"Nurse Ramath!" The old country doctor shifted in his desk chair to face her. He peered over the frames of his reading glasses. "I cannot accept that you, of all people, could be intimidated by this-"

"It's Mr. Suddeth this time. And you know what a violent case <u>he</u> was." She peered over her shoulder as if he might pop out from behind her. "Patterson is totally cowed. Says he won't stay where there's no future."

"That lummox!" Chalmers shot out of his chair, and approached the woman, who was a good foot taller than him. "I count on you to keep order around here. I cannot have the patients see you wetting your panties over some county charity case." He poked her with his index finger for emphasis. "Now, get Mr. Suddeth in here immediately. I want to examine him."

Nurse Ramath directed her six-foot two-inch frame towards the day room while Dr. Chalmers searched his shelves for his copy of the Diagnostic and Statistical Manual of Mental Disorders. "I could be yanking some six-year-old's tonsils." He began rifling through a lower shelf. "Six-o-clock cocktails at the club with Mrs. Chalmers instead of cold leftovers alone at seven-thirty."

Nurse Ramath reappeared in his doorway with a man looking more like Mr. Rodgers than a maniac. Wearing a blue Cardigan sweater, gray slacks and a pair of open-back house slippers, he was clean-shaven with neatly combed hair. Dr. Chalmers straightened, his mouth agape at the sight, but quickly regained his composure.

"Nurse Ramath, what is this? Where is Patterson? I refuse to examine this patient alone. It's unsafe."

"He's docile as a lamb." The nurse turned to leave. "See for yourself."

Chalmers circled Mr. Suddeth, giving him a wide berth. For his part, Suddeth watched with bemused curiosity as if it was the caregiver who had suddenly lost his mind. The doctor closed his door, never taking his eyes off the slightly built man.

"I must warn you, I carry a wireless panic alarm in my pocket, which I can activate at a moment's notice." The doctor patted a roll of lozenges in his coat pocket for emphasis. "Two strong orderlies will be here in seconds to subdue you and prepare you for electro-convulsive therapy."

"Sorry about the bite." Suddeth's voice was now unimposing.

Chalmers noted the new demeanor. He was talking to a different person. Still, the doctor observed the scar and stitch marks on his wrist as testimony of the patient's violent tendencies.

"I don't know what I was thinking." Suddeth shook his head.

"I know what you were thinking." The doctor circled back to his desk. "I've had years of training to know how you think."

"That's nice." He leaned against one of the tall bookcases. "Then what I'm about to do won't come as any surprise."

"What are you about to do?" Chalmers went for the lozenges out of reflex.

"I'm leaving."

"What?"

"I was packing when Nurse Ramath came by."

"You can't!"

"I can!"

"You hear voices.

"Not anymore."

"You think electrical outlets record your thoughts."

"Not these days."

"You can't form a coherent sentence."

"I'm forming them now." Suddeth looked in-control and relaxed.

"Well, I won't release you!"

"You don't have to. I've contacted my family and formed several coherent sentences for them. By this afternoon, my lawyer will be here with the papers." He moved to the door. "I'd love to stay, but I've got to get ready to go." Suddeth cracked the door open and then turned back. "You know the funny thing, Doctor?"

"No," Chalmers sighed. "What?"

"They think this is *your* doing." Suddeth laughed. "They think you're a miracle worker!"

Chalmers heard Suddeth's laughter disappear down the hall. Returning to his desk, he slumped into the leather chair. In all his years in practice, he'd never faced a crisis like this. Five patients cured in three weeks. It was intolerable. At this rate his Medicare income would evaporate. He could see Patterson's dilemma. This was not the economic model on which the modern mental health system was based.

The old psychiatrist stared out the window of his office, distressed at what he had just seen. Canada geese swam in the pond outside. He longed to join them, but decided to settle instead for sharing the spring air with them. Taking a ring of keys from his pocket, he used a small one to unlock the casement window and open it a crack. Scents of buds and blooms flooded in. He closed his eyes and inhaled the smell of awakening nature.

"See what I mean?" Nurse Ramath startled him.

"I see you let him access an outside line."

"Not me, Doctor." The nurse raised her hands in protest.

"No." Chalmers backed down. "I suppose this is *his* doing, too."

"Wouldn't surprise me at all." Ramath shook her head. "You know, Doris in housekeeping bumped into him the other day?" She lowered her voice to a whisper. "The piercings in her ear lobes were gone by the time she got home!"

"Humph. I'll thank you not to spread such rumors." Chalmers glanced through the stack of charts on his desk and sighed. "Find him, Nurse Ramath " The doctor waved his hand. "Bring him here."

The nurse departed without a word, leaving Dr. Chalmers to his own thoughts. He opened the top chart, but couldn't bring himself to give it due attention. He looked out at the pond, admiring the geese and their freedom. A quiet knock at the door brought him back.

"Here's our troublemaker." Chalmers turned to face a disheveled man in pajamas and bare feet. Probably in his late twenties, this patient had the wild hair and full beard that spelled an ideal case for the doctor. Chalmers could easily see him wearing a loincloth and hair shirt, baying warnings of imminent doom in the wild. Instead, here he was, spreading contagious rationality unchecked through the ward.

"You seek me and here I am," he sat on the leather couch in Chalmer's office as if he owned the place.

"Patient 3152." Chalmers drummed his fingers on the chart, wondering where to go next.

"I have a name," he smiled. "I came in with one."

"I know," the doctor frowned, "but to use it would only reinforce your delusion." He studied the man. Nothing imposing or outstanding about him, other than the fact he was found ranting on a street corner and brought to the doctor's sanitarium for evaluation. "I'm sure the authorities will eventually discover you're a missing person — or escapee — somewhere."

"Are you sure?"

In fact, the doctor wasn't sure at all. The only thing he could be sure of was that his income base was dwindling. "What I am sure of is that you are disruptive and uncooperative. The question is: what to do about you?"

"You could send me on my way."

"Yes-" The doctor's mind wandered out the window again. "I mean, no! I have a responsibility to the community."

"As do I."

"You?" Chalmers snorted. "I've run into many just like you."

"As have I with the likes of you." He smiled. "Keep me from my task and soon you and I will be the only ones here." Chalmers was forced to think. The man's quiet self-assurance was threatening.

"I'm going for the nurse." Chalmers left his office, and letting himself in the day room with a key, went straight to the nurse's station. He waited for the woman to finish a medication report.

"Did you want something, Doctor?" Nurse Ramath looked up.

"Yes." Chalmers was calm and deliberate. "Join me in my office for a moment, would you?" He turned to unlock the day room door.

"Anything wrong, doctor?" She followed closely.

"No, I just want your assistance with patient 3152." There was a noncommittal tone to his voice and an uncharacteristic slowness to his pace. He opened the door to reveal an empty office. "He's not here."

"I'll call the police." Nurse Ramath turned to go.

"I'll handle the authorities." The doctor dismissed her. "In a day or two," he said to himself.

Dr. Chalmers sat at his desk puzzling over the chart on his last patient. "Delusional," he read his own diagnosis, "with a deep-seated messiah complex," He paused to enjoy the breeze coming in from the open window. Taking a deep breath, Chalmers held the spring air in his lungs, then began to add a final note to the chart.

"While clearly out of touch with reality," he wrote, ignoring the pajama-clad figure walking across the pond as if it were frozen, "patient 3152 does not appear to be a threat to society or himself. Released on self-recognizance."

11

THE

CLEANING OF HILL HOUSE

"**H**oney, I'm home!" Stanley Jackson muttered to himself as he entered from the garage. Lately, it was a tepid testing of the waters instead of the call to action it once had been. He waited. There was no reply. He dreaded coming home.

With a sigh, Stanley set his briefcase down on the kitchen counter and looked around. Her "touch" was everywhere. All of his things were arranged in tidy piles. The dishes he used that morning were stacked by size in the sink. The wedding album that had lain open the night before stood closed next to the phone and its now neatly coiled cord. A dozen cards and letters Stanley dreaded answering lay unopened on the kitchen table, sorted by size and color.

She's getting worse, he thought, reaching for a Prozac, an unasked-for gift from his doctor. Stanley was still struggling to get out from under his own recent depression. He was sure the beeping answering machine held messages of sympathy and encouragement from people who had no grasp of his current situation. He might get to those this weekend if she would just cooperate.

Why can't she give it a rest? He asked himself. *You'd think for once the house would be clean enough for her.* He bit his lip. *And I'm the one on Prozac.* Stanley slowly shook his head and began to listen. It took him a moment, but eventually the faint sound of brushing directed him where to go. *She'll be sweeping until doomsday.* He walked softly through the dining room and into the living room, stopping at the archway. Stanley found her in the foyer, on all fours, collecting dirt with her hands from the carpeted treads of their circular staircase.

"There you are," he said softly. Pale and wasted, she didn't stir, but kept using her fingers to brush the dirt into a small pile. She was on the second tread from the bottom, with one left to go. Stanley wondered how long his wife had been at it like this. "Don't you hear me, Shirley?" he asked.

"Of course I hear you," she said without looking up or slowing the pace of her cleaning. "I'm not deaf, you know."

"I know you're not deaf, but you are very single-minded these days. Obsessive, one might say." Stanley wondered if any of his words registered with her. "Can't you give it a rest?"

She replied with a faint snort and increased effort.

"We do have a vacuum cleaner." He started for the hall closet. "I'm perfectly capable— "

"You?" She turned and looked at him with faint derision. "You'd miss ninety percent of it for sure. I'm sorry, Stanley, but you were never the cleanest person on the planet," she snickered. "I knew that when I married you." She went back to brushing the dirt with her fingers. "You could be more understanding. I'm just trying to maintain the status quo."

"You can't have the status quo. We can't go back. I love you with all my heart, but you make it much harder this way." Feeling the drugs kick in, he steadied himself on the balustrade.

The thought of seeking professional help had crossed Stanley's mind before. It was beginning to rise to the surface again. "I know how to operate a duster and a mop," he insisted. She made no effort to slacken her pace. He watched a moment, then added softly, "You know, you could do it this way for an eternity and still not be happy with the results. You need assistance."

"That may be, Stanley, but it gives me a purpose. Let me be, won't you?"

"I can't let it go, Shirley. This isn't good for either of us." He shifted closer to the stairs, trying to put himself in her line of vision. "Listen to me, won't you? You need to stop this. I can get you help. A cleaning service, for instance-"

She stared at him as if he had grown a second head. "They slack off when your back is turned, and never do it the way you want." She quickened her pace.

Stanley knew further conversation was pointless. She'd driven several cleaners out of the house already with her "helpful" fastidiousness. He opted for a new tactic. "I'm not happy here," he countered. "I don't know how else to say this, Shirley. I feel trapped in this house with you."

"Then go out, for goodness sakes!" She looked at him with a wan smile and shook her head. "I'm not keeping you here."

"But you are. You do." He dropped down on one knee, bringing himself to her level. "I couldn't leave you like this. This is wrong, Shirley. Very wrong. We *both* need to move on."

"'Til death do us part?" She shrugged her shoulders and started on the last tread.

"I wish..." he muttered.

"It's your anxiety, not mine. I'm quite happy staying at home. I've always loved this house. You're the one unhappy with the situation. Go. Have a life if you think it will help."

Sighing, he rose slowly, knowing he could never change her situation by himself. His considered other options. Professional help was what he needed. *Father Black,* he thought, *he must have some experience with this- Maybe she'd respond to him.*

The doorbell rang, causing them both to look up. A forty-ish woman in a cocktail dress was visible through the window in the front door. Made up for the visit, she carried something in her hands.

"Camile Cucheon!" Shirley scowled at the woman from the house on the corner. "You watch out for her, Stanley."

"She's married for Christ sake." Stanley spoke through gritted teeth.

"I don't care," Shirley huffed. "I don't like her." She rushed up the stairs, leaving him to face their neighbor alone.

"Hi Camile," he opened the door. "Nice to see you."

"Stanley," she gushed, not waiting for him to invite her in. "I saw you drive home, and brought you this." She handed him the covered dish. "It's still warm."

"That's nice of you, Camile." He wasn't sure what to do with it: leave it there or take it to the kitchen, so he opted to set the casserole down on the small captain's desk that stood in front of the stairs.

"I hadn't seen you lately and wondered how you'd been getting along." She paused and lowered her voice a little. "You must really miss home cooking right now."

"No doubt about that." He forced a grin, trying to lighten things up.

"Oh my!" Camile caught sight of the dirt piles on each of the stair treads. "We are having some cleaning issues, aren't we?" She stared at the piles, trying to comprehend.

"Yes, well-"

"Why don't you get me your vacuum," she turned back to him. "I'll-"

"No. Really. I can handle things, Camile." Stanley began to maneuver her towards the door. "I need to learn how to manage this myself anyway."

"Are you sure I can't help?"

"I'm sure," he nodded, pulling the door open. "This is something I've got to work out for myself."

"All right." She stepped outside. "But Stanley," she held the door. "Don't stay cooped up. It isn't healthy. We all want to help"

"I know, Camile." He could feel her look of pity, and steeled himself for her next words.

"We were all so shocked at Shirley's death. Anything we can do to help, you let us know."

"I will, Camile. I will." He tried to force a smile. "Thanks for the casserole." He closed the door to the faint sound of brushing.

12 REVENGE

OF THE FLYING MONKEYS

"Where's the game board?" Mr. Benge scanned the clutter on the kitchen table. Stacks of mail and newspapers were shoved haphazardly to the side. A golden retriever circled, his nose sniffing the edge of the tablecloth with hope. "You said we were going to play a game." The chair creaked under his weight as he shifted.

"It's a card game, Dad." Todd Benge was home from college.

"Jeez-oh-Pete! You dragged me halfway across town for a stupid card game?" Mr. Benge picked up the box. "I should've known." The box, about the size of a hardcover book, had a still of Margaret Hamilton and her minions from *The Wizard of Oz* on the cover. Ozian lettering said, "*Flying Monkeys* - A Game for Munchkins of All Ages!" Mr. Benge turned it over, his lip curled revealing an incisor. "At least it's smaller than *Trivial Pursuit*."

"Be grateful, Dear." Mrs. Benge, fresh from the dishes in the sink sat next to her husband. "Thinking games only upset you." She patted his wrist. "Randall!" She called over her shoulder. "Where is that boy?"

"In the bathroom again." Snickering, Todd shuffled half the cards.

"You're only doing half the deck." Mr. Benge complained. He started to pick up the remaining cards.

"Don't, Dad!" Todd slapped his father's hand away. "That's the Dungeon deck. You can't mix it with the Treasure deck."

"What? Are we keeping Kosher or something?"

"Lionel, just let Todd take the lead." Mrs. Benge called over her shoulder again, "Randall Benge, get down here now."

A muffled response came from upstairs, followed moments later by the sound of a toilet flushing. Todd snorted. "Told ya!"

"Why don't you deal while we wait for Randall," Mrs. Benge suggested.

"Why don't you play his hand, too, while you're at it," Mr. Benge added.

"Lionel!" Mrs. Benge gave her husband a look as Todd dealt two cards each to four places.

"Well?" Mr. Benge waited, then asked, "Are you going to finish dealing, college boy?"

Todd looked at his father as if the man had sprouted orchids from his nostrils. "Dad, that's all you get to start."

"Lucky it's not strip poker." Mr. Benge picked up his cards, frowning at them. "This could be one short round."

"Try and get into the spirit of the game, Dear." Mrs. Benge looked at her hand. "Oh, my!" She laid her hand face up on the table. "What are these?"

The two cards had cartoons drawn on them. There was a lot of printing, too. The first card had a picture of a donut-hole. The second was of a man in a green eyeshade and chewing on a pencil.

"Wow, Mom!" Todd spoke in hushed reverence. "You got a Munchkin and the Auditor of Redundancy."

"Is that good?" Mrs. Benge squinted at the cards.

"A Munchkin protects you from attack by a level six Threll! You can use the Auditor of Redundancy to rob an opponent of all his treasures."

"Oh." Mrs. Benge picked up her cards to study them. "That's nice."

"What did you get, Dad?"

"Are you nuts?" Mr. Benge clutched the cards to his chest. "I'm not giving away my hand."

"Dad, you've never played this before!"

"I'll take that risk." Mr. Benge laid the cards face-down in front of him.

"Have you done the face-off, yet?" Randy breezed into the room, plopped into his chair, and picked up his two cards.

"Nah," Todd tried to see his brother's cards. "Is your banana peeled?" He started to snicker.

"Why you-" Randy slammed his cards down.

"Randall Benge!" His mother interrupted. "Are you eating between meals? I've just gotten the corned beef and cabbage put away and you're snacking?"

"Mom!" Randy rolled his eyes as his brother sniggered.

"Face-off!" Todd began handing out small, colored pieces of plastic.

"What the hell is this?" Mr. Benge picked one up. It was multifaceted with a number on each of its triangular sides.

"That's a ten-sided die, Dad." Todd handed his brother a six-sided die. "You use it to track your level. Put the zero face up."

"Then why has he got a normal one?" Mr. Benge pointed at his younger son.

"That's to see who goes first."

Randy rolled a three; his father a five; Mrs. Benge rolled a four; and Todd rolled a two.

"Ha!" Mr. Benge straightened. "I go first."

"Not so fast, Dad." Todd handed the die his brother. "We throw out the high and low scores. They roll to determine who's first."

Mr. Benge's brow creased. "I think you made that up."

"Here." Todd handed him a small booklet. "It's all in the rules."

Mr. Benge began thumbing through the rule book as Randy and his mother faced off. "This reads like a tax form!"

"You go first, Mom." Randy set the die down.

"I do?"

"Lower number goes first," Todd confirmed. "Take a card from the pile on the right."

Mrs. Benge did so, and laid the new card face up next to the other two on the table. The new one had a squinty-eyed rodent drawn on it.

"The Mole of Malfeasance." Todd nodded. His father gave him a look.

"Is that good?" Mrs. Benge asked her son.

"That's a level-one irritant," Todd explained. "You discard him and take a card from the treasure pile."

"Don't forget to turn your die over so the one is face up," Randy added.

Mrs. Benge did so, laying a new card face up. It showed a tacky woman wearing junk jewelry. The heading read, "Nuclear Necklace."

"Cool!" Randy leaned in for a better look. "No one ever gets those this early in the game."

"Is it good?" Mrs. Benge asked, fingering her own necklace of pop-beads.

"Good?!" Todd's jaw dropped. "This triples your power. You're a level three. Plus you can obliterate someone with that." He turned his mother's die over then took a card from the dungeon pile. He flipped it face up. "Ha! Angry Ferret." He took three treasure cards and flipped his die to one.

Randy took a card and frowning, studied it for a while.

"Come on," his brother urged.

"Oh, all right." Randy flipped a card reading "Obsequious Mongoose" on the table, then added a card that read "Feast of

Famine" next to it. "I think that doubles it," he said, flipping his die to two and taking a couple treasure cards.

"At last!" Mr. Benge drew a card. He squinted at the three in his hand as time ticked by on the kitchen clock.

"Come on, Dad," Randy finally spoke.

"Can't you see this is a game of strategy?" he complained before throwing down a card. Todd and Randy both snorted.

"The Dweeb of Death!" Todd announced.

"So?" Mr. Benge crossed his arms.

"It means you give up another card in your hand and drop a level." Randy grinned.

Mr. Benge's neck started to redden. "That's not what it says on the card!"

"But that is what it says in the rules," Todd insisted. He quoted from memory, "'Any vocation card over three Elron's in value cannot be played in the first round without the Buddah-of-Butt-Kicking, or a Nebbish card worth at least two Trolls or three Elves.' It's in the rules, Dad." Todd waved the booklet at his father.

"Let me see that!" Mr. Benge snatched the book away, pouring over it as the game continued.

"Dad? Dad. Dad!" Randy shook his father's arm.

Mr. Benge looked up. "Cut it out! I can't read with you shaking me."

"It's your turn, Dear."

"What?" Mr. Benge stared at his wife.

"It's your turn," she repeated.

"I just picked up the rules," Mr. Benge groused.

"It's still your turn," she insisted.

"C'mon, Dad," Randy whined, "you're taking all the fun out of the game!"

"Fun," Mr. Benge harrumphed. "Like staying up late Christmas Eve to put your bicycle together. These rules read like the insert of a prescription of Via- Valium."

"That bike fell apart the first time I rode it." Randy stared accusingly at his father.

"It was the cheap, Korean construction."

"Let's don't revisit lost battles, Dear," Mrs. Benge interjected. "Pick a card."

"He started it." Mr. Benge began to draw a card from the Treasure stack, but Todd pointed him to the Dungeon deck. "Besides," Mr. Benge huffed, "the parts didn't agree with the instructions." He stared at the lone card in his hand. "I suppose since this is the only card I have, I've got to play it."

"You can pass, Dad," Todd cautioned.

"I wouldn't want to do that." Mr. Benge looked accusingly at Randy. "That might hold up the game." The instant he threw the card down, Todd slapped his forehead. Randy groaned.

"What!?" Mr. Benge looked around the table. Only his wife made eye contact. "Did I kidnap the Lindberg baby or something?"

Randy started, "Who's the Lind-"

"Randall," Mrs. Benge cut her son off. "Never mind."

"Dad!" Todd addressed his father as if speaking to the village idiot. "You played the Podiatrist of Perversity. That's a non-shielded envoy card. Everybody knows you can't play that before the first Pomeranian has been cast."

"Well, excuse me, Mr. College-boy." Mr. Benge pushed back from the table. "My parents didn't send me to some expensive community college, so I could learn stupid card games! I had to go out and earn a living, so you could come home every once in a while and remind me how hopelessly stupid I am." He got up to leave.

"Sit down, Dear." Mrs. Benge touched her husband's sleeve. "You don't want your sons to think of you as a quitter, do you?"

The statement caused Mr. Benge to stop. "Who says I'm a quitter?" He glared around the table. After so many years, the boys had learned to avoid his gaze at this point. "Just give me rules I can follow — the Reader's Digest version, for Pete's sake." He slowly settled into his chair. "Not some Abbott and Costello double-talk."

Randy opened his mouth to ask another question, but a look from his mother stopped him. "I guess it's my turn," Mrs. Benge said brightly. She picked up a card and thought for a moment before laying it down.

"Awright, Mom!" Todd said to his mother, "that entitles you to three treasure cards."

She started to reach for the pile when Mr. Benge grabbed her hand. "Just a darned minute!" He fished the bottom card out of the discard pile and held it up. "Tha's the same card as mine! The Deceased Dude."

"Dweeb of Death," Randall corrected.

"The first round has past," Todd explained as if his father was a child, "and Mom picked up a Nebbish card worth two Trolls and 3.5 Elves."

"And just where do you see the point value on these stupid things?" Mr. Benge squinted at the cards as his wife handed her glasses to him.

"You count the fingers showing on the left hand to get the whole number and the right hand gives you the decimal." Todd explained.

"Except with Elves," Randy corrected. "There, the right hand is the exponent of the logarithm."

"Now I need a slide rule to play this stupid game?" The veins in Mr. Benge's forehead began to pulse.

"Dad," Randy started, "What's a slide-"

"Lionel, Dear," Mrs. Benge interrupted, "I don't mind. If you want my points-"

"I do <u>not</u> need any help from <u>you</u>!" Mr. Benge straightened. "I can handle a simple card game." He picked up his hand.

"Of course you can, Dear." Mrs. Benge took her Treasure card. "Your turn, Todd."

"Uh, right." Todd looked at his Father warily before taking a card. He stared at it and appeared to blanch.

"Well?" Mr. Benge waited. "Got a bad card, huh?"

"I... Uh..." Todd looked to his mother for help.

Mr. Benge grabbed the card from his son's hand and threw it down. "Hah! The Foot Fetish Doctor card!"

"Podiatrist of Perversity." Todd corrected. "I guess I needed to shuffle-"

"Whatever." Mr. Benge recovered. "How do you like them apples, Mr. College? Now <u>you</u> lose a card!"

"No, Dad." Randy interjected.

"What?" Mr. Benge turned to his younger son.

114

"I played a Pomeranian with my last hand," Randy asserted. "You weren't paying attention. Todd gets <u>two</u> Treasure cards."

"I was too paying attention. And it has not escaped my attention what a stupid game this is." Mr. Benge rose from his chair. "I work all day. You'd think I could get some respect and relaxation when I get home. But no! I get some twisted little conspiracy in the form of a card game." He wagged a finger at his oldest son. "Don't think I'm not on to you. This is how you spend your time at community college. And you-" he turned to his younger son, "What was your last grade in math? You wouldn't know a logarithm if it fell on you in the forest."

"Now, Lionel—"

"Madam, the least you can do is keep order in this house while I'm earning the bread for your mouths. I'm going out for a smoke."

Mrs. Benge sighed as her husband stormed off then turned to her youngest son. "Randy, Dear…"

"I know. Mom." Randy rose and repeated what he'd heard so many time before, "go get the checkerboard."

"And try not to make it obvious you're letting your father win."

"I'll try," Randy said as he left.

Shaking her head, Mrs. Benge turned to Todd. "I knew this would happen," she sighed. "Thinking games only upset your father."

13 HOME

NOIR

It came with a knock at the door to my office.

"I need your help, Mr. Carlisle."

I knew the cry. I'd heard it before and it always meant trouble. I turned to the beautiful blonde standing in my doorway, the sun shining in her hair like the wax job on that yellow 'Vette I'd never be able to afford. *That's the price you pay for rampant orthodonture,* I reminded myself. "What can I do for you, Beautiful?"

"This is no time to be coy, Carlisle." She sauntered in, all business. "I can't find my car keys."

"Did you check your purse?" I was always good for reducing a complex issue to its essentials. You have to be in my business.

"Of course," she huffed. "What do you take me for?"

"Wouldn't you like to find out?" I thought I'd test her. Dames — the beautiful ones especially — are always looking for a come-on, except when they have a headache, which lately was often.

"For once, get your mind out of the gutter, Mr. Carlisle. Be serious," she snapped.

"I see." I rose to the gravity of the situation. "What is it? Hair appointment? PTA meeting? Tennis lesson?"

"Does it matter?"

I knew it did, but sometimes you have to let women keep their mystery, like what all the jars on the bathroom counter are for. And why you can't leave hair in the sink. It's part of their allure. "Did you check the house?" I went straight for the gut.

"Twice." She sank into my leather couch, and for a moment I wished I was a cushion. "What do you think I am? An idiot?"

I knew a direct answer wouldn't make the problem go away. I'd have to solve this crime, and fast! When trouble parks herself at your doorstep, ignoring her like a Jehovah's Witness with a handful of pamphlets won't make her depart. "All right," I said. "I'll take your case."

"Don't fall over yourself helping me." She rose to leave.

I could read the gratitude in her voice. "We can discuss my fee later, over dinner," I suggested.

"You'll be having frozen pizza. By yourself." She showed me that gorgeous backside. "I've got a library meeting."

Funny how she could predict outcomes like that. I looked around my office at all the critical work that wouldn't get done. My American League baseball card collection would have to remain un-catalogued. Once again, a beautiful dame takes a big chunk out of my life—the better part of an afternoon, for sure.

I could have back-tracked her footsteps, but there was no telling if she was being open with me. People forget things when it's convenient, like picking up the dry cleaning on the way home from work. A simple oversight, you might say. Not from her perspective. I knew that game well.

I decided to check my underworld sources. Unsavory characters, mostly, but they had eyes and ears and could observe things unnoticed by others. Little Rico was one of them. Small and wiry, he could disappear in a second when things got tough. Rico had an uncanny sense for that. If it was time to take out the trash, you were as likely to find him in Cucamonga as his usual haunts.

He typically hung out in his subterranean lair. I went straight for it and descended the bare wooden stairs as quietly as I could.

The corners were dotted with cobwebs. I was on the lookout for spiders. Somebody really should clean this mess up. Another case, another time, I said to myself.

I knew from past visits, the third tread from the bottom creaked. I was careful to avoid that, but I didn't see the Legos scattered on the second. I nearly fell over the railing and had to fight the urge to scream. Stepping on those things in bare feet was painful. Rico was getting clever in his old age.

Lights shone from the small room next to the furnace, another nemesis of mine, but we'll cover filter changes later. I could hear clicking noises and approached the door with caution. I peered in. He had his back to me — a big mistake. Rico was absorbed in surfing the web. "Looking up crime statistics?"

He jumped, but recovering quickly, clicked the browser's minimize button. That was OK. I knew all about the history file. My night was planned. "Whaddaya want?" His steel-gray eyes bored through me like a Tupperware container left on a hot burner. Crazy, but dames never forget stuff like that. I'd stick with Corelle in the future.

"Why Rico," I eased myself in, "a guy can't drop in to see his best buddy?"

"I'm not your best buddy!"

"Really? You're not still sore over the Petoskey caper, are you?" The silent surly look told me he was. I shrugged. Hazard of the job. "You do the crime, you serve the time, Pal." I hated turning him in, but sneaking out to play Frisbee after curfew is a serious offense in this town.

"Whaddaya want?" He repeated.

"Why Rico, I'm beginning to think I'm not wanted here." I eased around the room, but he kept his body between me and the keyboard. I definitely had my night cut out for me.

"I geeked out the litter box like you wanted. Why can't you leave me alone?"

"I will. Believe me." I held eye contact with him. Narrow and deep set under a uni-brow, his eyes revealed his true criminal nature. *Gets it from his mother,* I thought. "I just need a little information." I sat down, crowding his space. I could tell by subtle clues like the curl to his upper lip he hated it. Then again, it might have been that retching sound he made as he drew back. "I'm looking for a set of keys," I continued. "Perhaps you've seen them?"

"Keys? What would I know about keys?" He turned back to the computer. "I don't need no stinkin' keys! I don't drive."

He was right, of course. Only someone with a valid class-two or class-three vehicle operator's license could possibly have taken them. "You got a point there, Kid." I rose, ready to strike fear. "You're off the hook for now, but mind your P's and Q's. I'll be watching you."

I could tell by the way he didn't turn from the computer that I had him spooked. I headed up the stairs, out of his grungy hideout. I thought I'd better check in with my client. She seemed the anxious type. After a brief search, I found her in the laundry room.

"Do you have to leave your socks rolled up in a ball?" She hissed.

"I wouldn't know much about that, Sister." I stepped over a disgusting pile of rags, wondering, when was the last time I bought underwear? "I spoke with your friend Rico," I offered. "He wasn't much help."

"Of course not, you twit. He doesn't drive."

I loved the way she could cut to the chase. That's rare in dames. She came at me with a look of raw passion. I knew to keep the detective/client relationship professional — at least for now — and stepped out of her reach. "I'll be back when I've got more to go on, Dollface," I called as a box of dryer sheets hit the wall behind me.

That's a woman for you. Give her a decent over handed throw, she's with you to the tenth inning. This one was ballet and symphonies all the way. Rico came up cold. That left me one option. I headed uptown.

If Rico was coarse and crude, Johnny D. was smooth — too smooth. A ladies man, you could count on him being on the phone. If he wasn't on the phone talking to a skirt, he was out with one. If he wasn't out with one, he was getting ready to go out with one. I could make a tidy living just keeping track of his dolls. A lesser guy would have been jealous — not me. Let him keep his bimbos. His socks always matched, and they coordinated with his pants, too. I hated that!

I made for his penthouse digs. Up the stairs I crept to Johnny's place, only to find his door ajar. *Careless,* I thought. I could hear him occupied on the phone, so I decided to ease my way in. It was his usual passionate babble. He caught me out of the corner of his eye and clammed up.

"Gotta go," he whispered. "You-know-who is here." He hung up the phone. "Why Pops," he turned to me. "What a surprise."

Surprised as a nudist on a luge run, I thought. "Just here for some male bonding," I lied.

"Yeah, right, Daddy-O!" He wasn't buying it.

I had to think quick. "Is that a scratch on your ludicrous CD?"

"That's Lud-a-criss!" He turned to look.

It was just the opening I needed. "Gotcha!" I pounced on him, attempting a half-Nelson, but the back of his chair got in the way. I went for my tried and true backup: nougies, but Johnny D. was on to me. We struggled, then he threw me back and we rolled onto his bed. I landed on a wooden hanger. Doesn't anyone ever clean up after themselves? His mother was going to get a stern talking-to as soon as the excruciating pain in my back went away. Johnny D. landed on top of me and my eyes went wide. It was then I noticed the Rolling Stone cover of Christina Aguilera taped to his ceiling. Whoa, Mama! My pupils dilated and my mind numbed. I ceased struggling. He was fighting dirty. Whatever happened to wholesome posters like Farrah Faucett? I wondered as the room spun like a child-proof cap.

I had Johnny D. right where he wanted me. He must have sensed the futility of his situation, because he let up. "Whatsamatter, Pops?" He kneeled on the edge of the mattress, taunting. "Getting old?"

"Not as long as Grecian makes formula, kid." I sat up and pushed him back, but he landed on his feet. Youth and agility! Who needs it? I'd get him another time. He had the hanger advantage for now, anyway. I surveyed his digs. It looked like someone had ransacked the place. Looking for what? I wondered. *Another time, another case,* I thought. "I'd love to help you figure out who did this to your room, Johnny, but I'm on an investigation."

"I didn't think you were here to socialize."

I had to admire his cynicism. It was clear he'd worked long and hard to perfect it. I wondered where he found the time. I would have tested it further, but remembered I was charging a client by the day. I went straight for the jugular. "A mysterious and beautiful dame has retained me to locate something of hers." Johnny D. gave me a puzzled look. "A set of keys," I continued, "rare and valuable, with a Double Coupon Shopper barcode tag on them." I studied his face for a reaction. "Maybe you've seen them?"

His features remained impassive. "Nope. Haven't seen 'em."

It was time to throw a curve. "That's not what Rico says."

His blue eyes flashed anger. "That little weasel!" Johnny D. stiffened. "He doesn't know what he's talking about." Johnny pounded his fist in his hand. "Wait 'til the next time I see him..."

"Watch yourself, Johnny." I was intrigued at the prospect of an impromptu personal security job, but other tasks beckoned. "Just testing you," I explained. "Besides, I know who drove the getaway car in the Petoskey caper."

Johnny D's poker face melted away like a Hershey bar on a hot dashboard. She wasn't about to let me forget that one, either. So it got into the defroster vent. Big deal.

"You wouldn't!" Johnny shrank back.

"But I could." I inched toward him. "Now where are those keys?"

"I don't know, I tell ya."

I could see fear coming out of Johnny's pores. A deep cleaning acne pad with astringent would fix that, but I wasn't going to help him out of his jam. "Are you sure?" I gave my most penetrating reply.

"I swear." He seemed genuinely cooperative. "The last I saw, they were in the candy dish in the kitchen."

The candy dish in the kitchen. Why hadn't I thought of that? "Thanks, Kid. You just saved me hours of mindless detective work." I started out, and then turned to survey his room one last time. "Just a tip, Johnny. Get yourself another decorator. This Hurricane Katrina look is way passé." I left him to chew on that wisdom and headed for the kitchen.

"Just the beautiful dame I was looking for." I encountered my client coming out as I was going in.

"Can't talk now," she blurted. "I'm late."

"Late for what?" A good detective learns to ask the hard questions.

"My library meeting!" She gave me that beautiful profile.

"But I've solved your case!"

"Case? What case?" She looked at me as if I'd booked the Dixie Chicks for a Republican fundraiser.

I had to remember, after all, she was a bit on the ditzy side. "Your missing keys." For a brief second, I wondered if she was going to stiff me for another P. I.

"You mean these?" She waved a ring of jingling metal in my face.

"Yeah, those." A good gumshoe notices these small details.

"They were in the candy dish where I left them," she laughed. "Pizza's in the freezer. Follow the instructions on the box. And clean up after yourself! Get John and Rick to help."

As suddenly as she entered my life, she was gone with the slamming of a garage door and the sputter of a mis-tuned engine. I turned and sighed. That was my fate with dames. If there was a noise to check out or a spider to kill, they were all over you. But after the crisis passes. . . .

I made my way back to the office. Dinner would be a good thirty minutes away, given the need to preheat the oven. That left me with time on my hands. I looked at my American League baseball card collection, and the challenging job of cataloging them that lay ahead. Would it be by team? Year? Lifetime stats? I pondered for what seemed like an eternity. Then, with a look of determination, I knew which way I had to go: Body Mass Index.

125

14 LETTERS

FROM CAMP KOROWAI

JUNE 12

Daddy,

How could you do this to me? I hate this place! How dare you send me to fat camp! What if my friends find out? I'll be ruined! It was rotten of you to have my stepmother pretend to take me shopping to get me here. That was a dirty trick!

Come up here immediately and take me home, and I'll see if I can forgive you someday.

Janie

~ ~ ~

June 16

Dear Janie,

Your father wishes he could visit you at camp, but he has been very busy as of late. Indeed, too busy to even write. I'm sure you'll understand. Keeping your pony in the manner to which it has become accustomed costs a pretty penny.

You can be sure your father had your best interests in mind. If you don't mind my saying so, you _are_ a bit on the plumpish side. A camp like this could do you a world of good, if you would settle down and apply yourself.

You'll have an expensive debutante ball coming up in the fall. Wouldn't you like to look presentable for it? Think about it. The summer will pass sooner than you think.

Your stepmother,

Angela

~ ~ ~

June 20

Dear Daddy,

Answer me! This is an awful camp! What kind of place is this? There is no hiking, no horseback riding -— no activities at all. How am I supposed to lose weight? They let us eat snacks any time we want. Did you ook into this place at all?

The other kids are all brats. They are fat and obnoxious. I don't belong here. Why can't you get me a personal trainer? Marcie Sloan got one. They sent her home early yesterday and nobody batted an eye.

Come up this weekend and bring me home!

Janie

~ ~ ~

Dear Janie,

How your father wishes he could come up and see you. Unfortunately, he is busier than ever. So busy, in fact, that he is out until all hours and always taking private calls. I know the calls are private, because they hang up whenever I answer. Curious, isn't it?

I hardly ever see your father, it seems. He's working too hard if you ask me. I'm going to see what I can do to force him to take a long vacation.

Until then, he has asked me to handle all correspondence with you. I hope you don't mind. As your stepmother, I hope this gives us a chance to grow closer. Anyway, take care, Sweetie. The summer will be over before you know it.

Angela

~ ~ ~

Dear Daddy,

I know you are reading this. You are just too frightened or ashamed of how you tricked me to answer. Stop hiding behind my stepmother.

The food here is terrible. Every night is some greasy form of mystery meat: pot roast ala Duane, or meatballs Suzanne. The counselors all think this is funny. I don't care what they call it. The food is still crappy!

Nancy Weldon's family took her to Europe for the rest of the summer. Her dad got an assignment in Rome. They came and got her late last night. I heard a boy named Dean Something-or-other had to go home early because his mother got sick. Why am I stuck here? This is so unfair!

Janie

~ ~ ~

131

July 3

Dearest Janie,

It grieves me to hear how unhappy you are. Distraught as you seem to be, the pounds must be melting off. We'll have to go shopping for clothes when you get back.

I have had success in getting your father to take time off from work. I sent him up to the lake house for some fishing. He's been gone several days, and must be laying low because I haven't heard a peep out of him. His attorney has called several times, but I've stood firm and insisted that your father not be disturbed.

I'd love to hear more about your adventures at camp. Write again, soon. The new pool boy is here. I must supervise his work. I want the pool perfect before your father returns. Ta, ta.

Angela

~ ~ ~

Angela,

Where is my father? It has been almost a month. What is he doing? Where is he?

The counselors here are strange. They're as fat as the kids and could use a diet camp themselves. They stare at us all the time. It gives me the creeps. If this is fat camp, why aren't we exercising? They weigh us every morning, but they don't tell us the results. What gives? They are strange, really strange!

A couple more kids got to leave early. A girl in my cabin left in the middle of the night because her father was sick. Two days later, some boy was sent home for bedwetting. If that's what it takes, I can have a bladder problem, too.

The food is still terrible. I can't see why the counselors like it. They say it is an acquired taste. The kids hate it. Please tell my father I want to come home now!

Janie

~ ~ ~

July 11

Dearest Janie,

It is always a treat to hear from you. Your letters are one of the few bright spots of my day. It seems your father is still away fishing. Perhaps I should be concerned, but he needed the time to himself. His attorney calls twice a day as it is. I suppose he can be concerned for the both of us. I don't see what is so critical about your father signing a new will, anyway. The one he has now is perfectly good.

I have to admit, with you and your father gone, it is all too quiet here. There are days I wander through these huge empty rooms wondering what to do with myself. My only company has been Raul. Did I mention we have a new pool boy? I think you'd like him if you met him. He's young. I'm amazed at all the work involved in maintaining proper pH. It has given him quite a physique, not that I notice such things.

It sounds like you are having a wonderful time at camp, so I'll close. Raul will be here shortly, and I want him to show me how to clean the filters.

Angela

~ ~ ~

July 15,

Angela help me!

I want to come home now! I hadn't noticed how many campers had left. There are less than a dozen of us here. What is it with this place? Soon, there will be more counselors than campers.

The other kids have gotten very quiet. Some of them cry a lot and stay in their cabins all day. I guess I'm lucky. At least you write me. Some of the kids haven't heard anything from home since they got here. Kids are still leaving, but the counselors no longer bother to explain where they've gone.

I asked one of the counselors how the camp got its name, and he said it was named after a tribe in New Guinea and started laughing. Where is New Guinea anyway? Why is it so funny?

There are rumors going around. A couple of kids went hiking and found some bones in the woods. The counselors were mad that they wandered off. They said there were wolves in the woods and that the bones belonged to kids who strayed from camp. I think they made that up. They took the bones to the kitchen to clean the dirt off them. We all got watery soup for lunch as punishment. One camper swore there was a fingernail in his. Gross!

Please bring me home, Angela. Please, please, please! The counselors count us twice a day and still some of us disappear. I don't know why, but have this awful feeling time is running out for me. Please, Angela, please!

Janie

~ ~ ~

July 20

Dear Janie,

I wish the news here was good. It is just as well you are at camp. Your father has been gone far too long. His attorney has asked the sheriff to drag the lake. They found your father's fishing boat drifting empty and suspect something bad has happened. I'm beside myself with worry.

I'm going to Cancun to wait. It is dreadful here, and Raul has offered to go along so I won't be lonely. Isn't that sweet? Did I mention our new pool boy is a whiz at massage? I have these terrible knots in my neck I want him to work on.

Speaking of lonely, with you and your father gone, I thought your pony was feeling neglected. I had it sold. I'm sure you won't mind. It is one less worry for your father and I know you'd want what is best. Besides, you can always get another pet. Goldfish are nice!

I'm glad things are going well for you at camp. I just got a call from your counselor. You're very popular it seems. She said you were a big hit at dinner. They also say you're nothing but skin and bones. That's wonderful news! I knew this camp would change you for the better. I have to laugh, Janie. I warned you your summer would end too soon.

Deliciously yours,

Angela

AS EASY AS

FALLING OFF A LADDER

The roof, the ladder and I had a disagreement a couple of months ago. The ladder took the side of the house and I lost the argument. To make matters worse, the driveway refused to meet me halfway. That's how I wound up in the den, my knee propped up with a bag of frozen lima beans on top of it. Frankly, I prefer peas. Limas require longer cooking times and more seasonings. But, as it was either that or an opened can of concentrated orange juice, I went for the limas.

You may ask how this argument started in the first place. It was all the chimney's fault. We live in a Colonial Williamsburg style home. We had a Colonial Williamsburg roof and chimney until last month when the water heater started acting up. It began dripping from its drain spigot. To me, a minor case of water heater incontinence is no big deal. My wife thought otherwise. It was 25 years old (that's three-and-a-half in dog years); OK for a dog, but apparently at death's door for a major household appliance.

Replacing it was easier said than done. The water heater had gotten very cozy with the basement furnace. So cozy, that the furnace, water heater and chimney stack were all touching each other — a mechanical ménage à trois, you might say.

To extract the water heater from this relationship meant unhooking the gas and electrical from the furnace. This was how two different companies came out to make estimates and see this mess for themselves. They took many digital photos to share with others back at the office. One firm quoted us nearly two grand and said we would need a flue liner. The other said we didn't need one and claimed a mere $1,300 would do the job, though they did use a picture of our installation as a "how not to" lesson for their installers.

We went with the latter company, but not before the wife specked out a high-efficiency water heater. She didn't want to fall prey to the rising cost of oil. I didn't have the heart to tell her the water heater actually uses natural gas, but no matter. That added a few hundred to the estimate.

Monday rolled around as did the plumber at about 8:00 AM. The water heater-ectomy went OK. He was able to reconnect the furnace, but not before replacing all the gas valves-something about today's building codes: anything you touch, you upgrade.

The new water heater was moved over to the opposite side of the furnace, a little more than a foot away. If the furnace were dating your daughter, this would apparently be an acceptable distance to even the strictest parents. OK, it required new gas lines and water lines — no big deal. But then there was the venting. High efficiency water heaters don't go through the chimney; they go out through the side wall — some thirty feet and no more than three 90° bends in our case. This meant lots of four-inch PVC and a hole drilled through our brick wall.

Did I mention that the labor for this was by the hour? Did I mention the second guy showed up around ten with the new water heater? He also brought a flue liner. That's right. Now that the water heater had its own means of egress, the furnace had the chimney all to itself. Rather than allow exclusivity, code required that the chimney have a stainless steel flue liner for company. Wasn't that what this company told us we didn't need?

Of course after fussing with it for thirty minutes, the installer decided the liner wasn't long enough. Plumber number two took an hour and drove back to the shop for a flue liner extension. It seems no matter what it is; guys can't be honest about length. By the middle of the afternoon, I would go down to the basement every half hour or so to check. I felt like Captain Kirk, dropping by engineering to beg Scotty for more warp speed. Anyway, by six that night, the two plumbers were adding up hours and parts and I was beginning to feel as welcome as Geoffrey Dahlmer at a Boy

139

Scout jamboree. In the end, it cost us nearly two thousand dollars. Funny, the high estimate was...

So how is it the chimney's fault I wear a $200 brace? If you stepped into my front yard, you would have seen my Colonial Williamsburg chimney with a shiny stainless steel mushroom sticking out the far right flue. I'm no expert on early American colonists, their architecture or their furnaces, but I'm pretty sure they didn't have stainless steel mushrooms popping out their smokestacks.

In my frustration, I did something I'd never done in all my years as a homeowner: I climbed on top of my roof. The lowest part of my roof is a mere six feet off the ground; the highest part might be thirty feet or so, but the fact is I can reach at least one part of my roof with a stepladder. That inspires confidence, false confidence, but confidence nonetheless. By the way, a Colonial Williamsburg roof, if it is going to have any authenticity, will be made of real cedar shakes. I am proud to say, earlier that summer, we had our Colonial Williamsburg shakes repaired and sprayed with a slick-looking roof treatment.

My son climbs the roof all the time, so why shouldn't I? Before I sold the house, I promised myself I would go up and see the graffiti he painted on the flat part of the roof over his bedroom. Why should passing planes be the only ones to see his genius? The painter who did our house last summer said it was a must-see point on the tour.

Our roof slopes at a forty-five degree angle. It can be a tricky climb, but I got all the way to the top with a can of spray paint, just like my son. I did my job, caught his art show, and made it down without a hitch.

140

From the ground, my silver mushroom had turned Rust-o-leum brown, a nice brown, but it was still a mushroom. I thought about it a whole week before I decided topping the whole chimney-thing with a rectangle of half-inch wire mesh would soften the look and keep out foraging squirrels. I took some metal shears, a roll of galvanized mesh, and my trusty step ladder and started up again.

The only difference between now and the week earlier was the rain that fell the night before. If dry cedar is treacherous, the wet stuff is dangerous. After nearly sliding off the garage, I decided to leave things to the pros. I shoved the shears, let the roll roll off and eased my way back to the ladder. I had one foot on, but it must have been the slippery one. On the way down my other leg caught in the rung and twisted.

I had a short fall perhaps, but it thrilled my audience anyway. The people from across the street paused only to score my dive then ran over and helped me into the house. Their visiting sister-in-law, a nurse, suggested limas as the main course. Nutty in flavor, they were a suitable accompaniment to the crow I would be eating later that night.

Two doctor visits later, I now know the knee brace I was wearing wasn't expensive enough. Silly me. I was treating a $200 wrench with a $20 brace. As a bonus, I also got a new lightening rod. This stainless steel flue liner, protruding from the highest point on my house, grounds out to the furnace in the basement, which is conveniently connected to every inch of ductwork, gas, electrical and even plumbing in our house. Lucky? And now I'm in plenty of hot water.

About a week after the water heater was installed, we had a cold snap and discovered neither of our furnaces would work.

141

Yes, we have two. Don't ask. We called the water heater installers in to check the first, thinking they might have broken it. They didn't. A nearby lightning strike burned out its circuit breaker. We paid for the call. We called in the original company, the "high" bidder to repair the second furnace. It needed an expensive part. "Oh, well. Might as well buy a service agreement for both furnaces," they suggested. "You'll save money and get free pre-winter checkups." That came to $600.

A month later we took them up on their offer. The furnace they worked on was fine. The furnace that was chummy with the water heater wasn't so lucky. It had a cracked heat exchanger. As that could allow carbon monoxide into our house, off went its gas and electric. In went the order for a high-efficiency replacement.

Several days later, two more installers and a small furnace showed up to the tune of four thousand dollars. Being efficient, this furnace vented out the back wall of the house. The water heater and big furnace had taken up all the good places on the side of our house. Another new hole cut in our brick and couple of cutouts in our plaster ceiling later and it was in. And the offending flue liner? Now totally unnecessary! The installers pulled it out as a favor before they left.

I can hardly wait until spring when they come back to inspect our outside air-conditioning unit.

DINOSAUR

DAYS

"Mrs. Triceratops!" A melodious cry
Rang out of the forest and into the sky.
A lumbering reptile turned around for a look.
As the speaker approached, the trees nearby shook.

Her hide, though quite rough and a little bit porous,
Was still in good shape for an old Stegosaurus.
An officer, once, in a reptile sorority,
She carried herself with an air of authority.

"My Dear, you've been missed," said the worried old soul.
"And you haven't been seen at the watering hole
In a coelacanth's age. And I thought I should see
If things with you aren't as they oughtn't to be."

Though nonplused at the query, the other replied,
"Well, my Dear, if I answer, I hope you won't chide,
But to keep to one's self isn't really a crime
And the little ones here consume all of my time."

Then she craned her head down to peer just past her legs
Where a hole in the ground held a large clutch of eggs.
"Myrtle sounds croupy," she said with a frown,
"And Dennis looks speckled- a little too brown."

"You fret too much, Dear!" The old reptile observed.
"It is bad for new moms, and the wee ones aren't served
Much by worrisome chatter and hovering about.
Go talk to your husband. You need a night out!"

"Ugh, that jerk?" The triceratops rolled her huge eyes.
"Every night it's the same: he goes out with the guys.
I've reached a conclusion, for what it is worth:
I'd trade you my tail and these eggs for live birth!"

"Oh, my Dear, that's mammalian!" Her matronly chum
Clucked her tongue and then added, "they're furry and dumb!
They've no future at all, really pitiful creatures.
I'd never give up my reptilian features."

"Be that as it may," mother dinosaur sighed,
"It's the tension of waiting I cannot abide."
"You'll see it's soon over," her good friend retorted.
"They grow up too fast," the old matron reported.

144

"Why, my little Eggbert," the old one went on,
"If allowed, would do science from dusk until dawn.
His theory (he tells me, quite free of restraint):
We're descended from fishes! Now, isn't that quaint?"

As the two reptiles chortled, the ferns and palms shook,
And a small pterodactyl swooped down for a look.
"Ah, these children," the stegosaur wiped a small tear,
"Are comical often, but most when sincere."

Her friend slowly nodded and began to respond,
When a call of "Yoo-hoo" floated in from the pond.
"Oh, great," said the old one, "it's Ms. Brontosaurus.
She'll make us extinct, if she doesn't first bore us."

"Why, Selma," the old one applied her best smile.
"Where have you been keeping yourself all this while?
You're looking quite svelte. You must share how it's done.
If I'm right, by my guess you have dropped half-a-ton."

"Two tons-and-a-half," the young brontosaur grinned,
"And another half-ton every time I break wind.
It's a novel approach, though a bit indecorous,
As it does tend to fell groves of trees in the forest."

"No doubt," said the stegosaur, hardly conforming,
"And does it adversely affect global warming?"
"That panic-strewn nonsense? I couldn't care less.
The work of some herbivore wonk, I should guess.

"But listen, I'm here with a gossipy tale:
A tyrannosaur family moved in up the trail!"
"Oh, no!" The triceratops cried with alarm.
"Our neighborhood's suffered irreparable harm!"

"They're snappish and lazy," the stegosaur whined.
"Wherever they move, nesting prices decline.
You can't trust a carnivore, that's very plain.
How will our society weather such strain?"

"In our situation, there's no need for tears.
Our kind has existed for thousands of years."
The brontosaur sat on her keester to park it.
"As a hedge, though, my own nest has gone on the market."

"A prudent precaution," the stegosaur nodded.
"I'll sell mine as well. I don't need to be prodded."
"Oh, dear!" The triceratops' grimace was striking.
"And I'd just arranged all these rocks to my liking."

The three sat in silence a moment or two,
The triceratops wondering what she should do,
When everything brightened, at least in the sky,
When high overhead a huge object zoomed by.

They watched in amazement, each locking their eyes on
This hot massive shape as it reached the horizon.
"That's odd," said the brontosaur, "I don't recall
Their predicting a meteor shower at all-

"Not during the day," and she would have said more,
But her next observation was masked by a roar.
Or was it a bang? No, a boom! That was it.
And just for good measure, the earth shook a bit.

"My, that was loud," cried the old stegosaurus.
"Let's hope that's the last," they all muttered in chorus.
And nervously watching and waiting for more,
The eldest observed, "Well, it's just as before."

But a silence ensued. They continued to harken
For sounds as they noticed the sky start to darken.
"It's looking like rain," the brontosaur twittered.
"I'd best to my nest as my wee ones aren't sittered."

"Toodle-loo," said the Stegosaur, watching her go.
"She's a breeder of worry and doom, don't you know."
"I wonder," triceratops asked, "Is there basis
To think what just happened has ruined our stasis?"

"Stuff and nonsense," the Stegosaur huffed, "Just a storm
Blowing in from the sea. Feel the air growing warm?"
"And awfully dusty," triceratops sneezed.
"Yes, well I should be getting on, too," her friend wheezed.

And lumbering off at a pre-glacial pace,
The stegosaur turned to observe her friend's face.
"Now don't let this gloomy sky fill you with sorrow.
The sun will return. There is always tomorrow."

17 THE

LISTENER

'Is there anybody there?' he said.
But no one descended to the Traveler;
No head from the leaf-fringed sill
Leaned over and looked into his gray eyes,
Where he stood perplexed and still.
But only a host of phantom listeners
That dwelt in the lone house then
Stood listening in the quiet of the moonlight
To that voice from the world of men:

- From "The Listeners" by Walter de la Mare

Norman Updike was a strange bird. But then all of his people were. Mention the name Updike 'round these parts and you'll think our winters are hot compared to the cold stares you get. No one much cared for them. A proud and standoffish lot they were before the trouble came. Not a one of them left now. Folks here are just as happy things are that way, too.

They claimed to be noble Scots from the time of William the Conqueror. I wouldn't know about that. Not much nobility there that I could see. They sure acted like they were royal; owned all the mills 'round here until the work moved south and then overseas. Any poor girl working there was subject to whatever whims one of them Updikes might have. Thought they owned the town, they did.

Like most anything, sooner or later things decline. So it was with the Updikes. Nathaniel never came back from the second world war. That left his brother Avery, Norman's father. What a drunken sot he was! No one knows who Norman's mother was. Talk is that it was some poor servant girl. Died in childbirth. If that was true, Avery didn't mourn a second — not that he had it in him to.

It was the matriarch Lydia who took charge. Old lady Updike was the lynchpin of the family. Behind her back, folks used to call her the "iron maiden." Whatever happened to Norman's poor mother, you can be sure Lydia Updike was behind it.

Took it with her to her grave, she did. Left poor Norman obsessed with findin' out. I suspect if Norman wasn't the last of the Updike line, he'd of been quietly put up for adoption, and the mother paid off and sent packin'.

Myself, I think Norman's mother died in childbirth on account of things my father said. For forty years, my father was the sexton of the Episcopal church here. I took over for him when he retired. We New Englanders are big on tradition. Besides cleanin' and keepin' the candles from burnin' down the chapel, it's the sexton's job to open and close graves. Many a time, my father warned me to watch where I dug. He wouldn't tell me where, though. I'd ask, but he always got this look on his face. "Don't ever cross Lydia," he'd say, but she was long dead by then.

It was '46 when Avery drank himself into a stupor. They found him frozen to death up at Shaw's Mill. Lydia was never the same after that. Took the wind out of her sails, it did. To lose two sons so close together. She probably would have died then, but she had her grandson to live for, poor devil. Who'd want Lydia Updike's undivided attention?

Norman sure didn't, I can tell you. As soon as he was of age, he enlisted and went off to fight in Korea. Maybe a year-and-a-half into his stint, Old Lady Updike died. The Army let him out early to clean things up. The few servants she had left, he let go. There he was, knockin' 'round that huge empty house by himself.

Folks say that's what made him strange. Talk was that house was haunted. Poppycock! There's folks livin' in it now. The townsfolk don't know the half of it. Norman came back from the war that way. There he was — the last Updike — little power, no livin' relatives, alone in a crumblin' house and a burnin' curiosity about who his people were. And by that, I mean his mother's side. He had more exposure to the Updikes than he could handle.

I should have stopped him that October morning, that morning I saw him in the church yard. All-Saints is one of the oldest churches in these parts. Some two hundred fifty-odd years ago, Reverend Ephriam Updike, a recent graduate of the Boston Theological institute, canoed down the Nashua river until he was stopped by the rapids at Hollis Depot. He thought he would civilize the native population. Too bad for him, they had other ideas.

The young Reverend was the first to be buried in the church yard. In fact, there was no church at the time. He was buried in the spot where the Peqwauket felled him with a tomahawk. Might have been the Narragansett. Anyway, the preacher's rich kin from Boston decided he should be buried in hallowed ground. So they hallowed it after the fact by building a wayside chapel there.

It was later Updikes who built it up into the stone edifice it is today. They took their fair share of the cemetery plots as a result. Anything close to the church is theirs. Bein' rich enough to buy a bishop, for a long time they chose the ministers, too. Yup, the Updikes settled in for a long stay. Too bad religion never rubbed off on them. Their love of drink always took priority. Old man Updike died of cirrhosis, they say. That's not official, you understand. The job of sexton is a semiofficial position. My father had an obligation to see the death certificate. He'd never talk about it, but he knew the real cause.

Anyway, Norman come back from Korea. He must have been one of those mine sweepers. Early one October morning, when frost was on the grass, I looked at the church yard and there he was. Norman was out there wearin' headphones and carryin' one of them mine detector things from the war. He was walkin' back and forth over the graves. I had a touch of rheumatism that mornin', but I had to go see what he was up to.

"Won't find any land mines out here, Norman," I says. Well, you should've seen him jump. Thought he would leap over one of them Civil War monuments.

"You shouldn't sneak up on somebody in a cemetery." He looked like he'd been caught. He slid one of the earpieces back to listen better.

"You don't think the Commies have been booby-trappin' our buryin' grounds, do you?" I asked.

Norman looked... Old? Like he'd done a lot of growin' up before he was ready to. Maybe he'd seen something over there he wished he hadn't. "Just a little research, Crenshaw," he winked. Norman didn't call you by your first name. That would've meant you were his equal. His grandmother taught him that lesson very early on. "Haven't you got some candlesticks to polish?" He snickered.

"Got to make sure these graves don't get disturbed." I answered. He might be an Updike, but I wasn't givin' him any ground.

"Why, Crenshaw," he cocked his head back, studyin' me, "what do you take me for?" He smiled. "I'm just doing some research. Besides, somebody's already been here."

"Been here?"

"Over in the new section. Vandals." Norman pointed to the far corner of the churchyard, towards the creek. It hadn't been used for buryin' until recently on account of the floodin' the stream tends to do every spring. "Somebody's knocked a couple of headstones over." He slipped his earpiece back over his ear as I turned to look. "You're slipping there, Crenshaw. Your old man would've caught that."

I heard his laughter fade as I rushed toward the stream. Cyrus Newton's stone lay face-down on his grave. It was thick Vermont granite. It would take a jack and winch to lift it in place. I'd helped put it in when I was seventeen. Took four strong men to set it. I couldn't imagine how many scrawny teenagers it took to topple the thing.

I shook my head and turned to see Emmet Tilghman's monument lyin' on its back. One of the stone urns on top had cracked off when it fell. That did it. I was callin' in the constable. This was more than a simple prank.

Odd that those two stones should've fallen to vandals. Talk was Emmet had a thing goin' with Cyrus' wife. It was all over town, but Cyrus never knew. We New Englanders can be discreet that way. Cyrus went to his grave ignorant. I wondered how his wife Vera, now in her eighties, would take the news.

I turned to look for Norman Updike, but he was gone. Must've ducked down Spring Street, headed for home. Wasn't even seven-thirty and already my mornin' was ruined. I went to the back of the church and let myself in through the basement door. All-Saints has been added to over the years. A classroom building from the 30's was the last thing done. My desk was in the boiler room underneath. Not much light down there except a sixty-watt bulb. The deacons weren't about to spring for a hundred-watter. Grungy down there, too.

I'd planned on gettin' ready for the season's first delivery of coal. Instead I sat down at my desk, an old door propped up on two squat filing cabinets, and stared at the cup of cold mornin' coffee. Disgusted with the taste, I dumped it down the floor drain and picked up the phone. Wasn't more than two rings when Sylvia down at the village office picked up.

"Oh, Weldon, it's you," she says like I'm a long lost friend. "Isn't it awful about Vera?"

"I'm sure it is, Sylvie," I answer. "Put me through to Constable Dodd, would you?"

"I wish I could, Weldon," she twitters, "but he's over at the Newton place. Probably for most of the morning."

"Well, have him stop by All-Saints or call me when he gets in." I started to hang up.

"I guess you'll want an early start," Sylvia says.

"Early start for what?" I stared at the calendar from Ferguson's Hardware on the wall. Nothin' set for the week except a Saturday mornin' quiltin' bee.

"Why, digging Vera's grave, of course," she clucked.

"All right, Sylvie, what happened?" I asked, though the story was comin' anyway.

"I shouldn't tell you official business, Weldon, but you're the sexton. You'll find out anyway."

"Go on, Sylvie."

"Well, you know Vera was pretty much bedridden." Sylvia's voice took on a conspiratorial tone.

"Ayup. Since her stroke last November," I agreed to keep things movin'.

"Every morning at six-thirty that woman from Elder Care over in Leyton comes over to bathe her and get her breakfast."

"Big hulk of a gal," I added.

"Well, she gets there and the back door is ajar. So she goes in to find everythin' torn up, like there was a struggle."

"Uh huh," I said, wishin' now I hadn't poured that coffee out.

155

"She calls for Vera, but gets no answer. Vera's not anywhere in the house. So the Elder Care lady goes to the kitchen to call for the Constable. And that's when she sees it."

"Sees what?" I ask after the pause. Sylvia knows how to milk a story. Village politics was a good fit for her.

"She looks out the kitchen window and sees Vera tangled up in the clothesline like a fly in a spider web." Sylvia paused again. "Weldon, her feet weren't touching the ground at all. Nobody can figure out how she got out of the house and twisted up like that."

"I'm sure Constable Dodd will figure it out. Have him stop by, would you Sylvie?" I hung up, disgusted. Now things were much worse. I had to dig a grave, but first I had to get those stones back up before the funeral. So much for a week's lead time.

The Ketcham brothers ran the local Standard Oil station. They had a wrecker we'd used to straighten out stones that had been leanin'. Gettin' the truck in between the headstones would be tricky, but we'd done it before. I called, and for $50 got them to agree to come out in the mornin'. I'd explain the bill to the deacons after the funeral.

I headed back out to mark Vera's grave figurin' I might as well get a head start. The Detmer boy would help with the diggin'. Strong back, that boy has. I'd argued for a backhoe like they have in Pickford, but the deacons....

Tommy Detmer was a good kid, a fullback on the high school football team. Had a full athletic scholarship to Hampshire College, but Laurie Metcalf turned up pregnant.

156

That cut his ambitions short. He's married and livin' in a trailer on his folks' farm. Winters, he runs a snowplow. Summers, well, he does what he can, what with a kid and all: paintin' and other such odd jobs as he can find.

I started towards the far end of the cemetery, a tape, four stakes and a mallet in hand. The day had warmed up and my jacket was back in the boiler room I paused under a large willow, where a marker of pink granite lay by itself on the bare ground. The Detmer boy had dug this grave by himself — refused to be paid, too. A withered bouquet of lilacs, left the week before, lay next to the stone.

Lichen was startin' to grow in the rough places on the marker. I'd come back later with some bleach and a wire brush to clean it. Still, you could read the inscription: Emily Crenshaw, beloved wife, 1917-1945. She died in February, the same week as the Ames boy was killed over in Iwo Jima.

We'd tried so hard to have a child. It meant a lot to her, the last of three sisters to get pregnant. She thought she was expecting and made an appointment that week. The doctor called it "deep vein thrombosis," a fancy way of sayin' blood clot. Not that it was any consolation. She was still dead when I found her. Eight years gone now.

"Hunting vampires?"

"Huh?" I started.

"The stakes and mallet." Ed Dodd pointed to the objects in my hands.

"Uh, yeah," I acknowledged. "I was just goin' to mark—"

"Vera's grave," he finished. "That Sylvia," he shook his head. "What was it you wanted to see me about?"

"Over here." I led Constable Dodd over near the creek.

He whistled, seein' the overturned stones. "You got your work cut out for you."

"You do, too," I reminded him. "This might have somethin' to do with your problems this mornin'."

"Ayup. It might," he agreed, squattin' to examine Cyrus Newton's stone. "This is, what?" he asked. "Seven hundred pounds?"

"Rock of Ages finest," I confirmed.

Ed stood, tipping back his hat. "Had to be a gang of kids," he concluded.

"Yup," I agreed, "no pry marks on the base."

Somethin' caught Ed's eye. He walked a short way back towards the church and stopped. I followed and was about to ask what was up. Then I saw it. "Jesus!"

"Jesus H.," Ed agreed.

"How did that happen?" I ran my fingers over the crack that zig-zagged down the middle of Lyman Norbert's monument. Lyman was a mean little cuss. Wasn't but twenty-three when he was killed. A fall down the stairs broke his neck. Left him pretty battered, too. His missus, a pretty little thing, had a child on the way. Can't imagine how she put up with his

158

drinkin' and carousin'. Lyman was three sheets to the wind when he took his final trip, so to speak. Not too long after, his wife Eileen took up with Clancy Garrett, the clerk at the A&P. They got married and he accepted her child as his own. Things turned out all right after that.

I remember they had trouble with the lowerin' mechanism at Lyman's funeral. His coffin didn't seem to want to go down. Deke Barbour, the local undertaker, fiddled with the thing 'til the catch finally released. Lot of grace under pressure that man has.

"Doesn't look like anyone struck it." Ed Dodd circled the stone. "Got any idea when this happened?"

"Truth be told, Ed, I hadn't noticed anything wrong when I was by here this mornin'."

"Notice anybody around?" He pulled a pack of Camels from his shirt pocket and grabbed a cigarette with his lips. He offered me one.

"No thanks," I declined. "Been tryin' to quit."

"Suit yourself." He slid the pack into his pocket and took out a battered Zippo. He lit the cigarette and took a long draw. "So, things pretty dead around here?" he grinned.

"Well, Norman Updike was out here this mornin'," I offered.

"He see anyone?" Ed closed his eyes and blew a stream of smoke. It danced and spiraled over Lyman's grave before a sudden breeze carried it off.

"Not that he said." I decided I'd have to break it to Lyman's widow, even though she might not want to do anything about it.

"About when was he here?" Constable Dodd absently flipped the lighter open and closed.

"Dunno. Probably seven, seven-thirty." I glanced back at the other two headstones.

"Wonder what was he doin' up at that hour?" Dodd flipped an ash on the grave and returned the cigarette to his lips.

"Can't really say." I was startin' to want a smoke, so I moved upwind. "He had one of those mine detector things, though."

"A metal detector?" Dodd pulled out the cigarette and exhaled towards me.

"I guess that's what it was." I looked back to where I saw him this mornin'. "I hope he's not plannin' on robbin' any graves."

"Shouldn't have to." Ed flicked another ash. "Lydia left him pretty well off, even after her temple to the dead." He pointed over his shoulder with his thumb towards the granite mausoleum near the church. We'd had to relocate a couple of graves to get it in. It was big enough for six, if you preferred layin' down for eternity.

There was a squawk from the radio in his patrol car. He dropped his butt on the ground and crushed it with his boot. "Better go see what Sylvia wants. At least you've got a day or two to straighten things out. The coroner's got Vera over in

Leyton for the next day or so. Give you a head start on her grave."

"I suppose," I said, followin' him back to his patrol car. "Any idea what happened?"

"Dunno, but she looked like Peter Pan with rigor mortis, tied up in the clothes lines like that." Constable Dodd shook his head. I turned back to the church to call Lyman's widow.

As I suspected, she weren't much inclined to do anything about the gravestone. She did say there was another kid on the way. I congratulated her and Clancy. They were movin' right along as a family. I had to suppress the thought of my own Emily.

~ ~ ~

Next mornin', I was up early on account of the Ketcham brothers bringin' their wrecker over to reset Cyrus' and Emmet's stones. A frost coated the grass, and the air was crisp with cold as I walked to the church. My breath left a trail of steam like a human locomotive. Eli and Hank Ketcham were waitin' with the tow truck when I got there.

"What's with old Norman?" Hank, the older of the two, greeted me.

"Norman?" I asked, shakin' Hank's hand.

"Norman Updike," Eli nodded in acknowledgement.

"He was here again?" I asked.

"Wanted to ask him what he was up to, but he took off like a scalded cat when he seen us." Hank climbed into the cab.

"Had some sort of thing he was wavin' over the ground." Eli stepped back to direct Hank with the truck.

"Oh." I moved out of the way as Ed signaled Hank to back up. "I gotta have a talk with him."

"Good luck with that," Eli grinned.

The three of us made quick work of settin' the stones. I paid the Ketchams cash. The transaction would show up on the church's books. I couldn't say the same for theirs.

Tommy Detmer came by about noontime, full of news. Clancy and Eileen Garret's house caught fire last night. Both adults and the child were killed. Fire chief couldn't be sure, but thought Clancy was smokin' on the couch and fell asleep. That would make three more graves to dig, and that meant more money for Tommy. No wonder bad news made him happy.

We talked about that and poor Vera. Got on to what kind of president Eisenhower might make over Stevenson. I said any man who couldn't keep his shoes fixed shouldn't be trusted to run the country. Tommy nodded, but I suspect he was a closet Democrat. Kept whistlin' "Happy Days Are Here Again" as he dug.

We finished up about four-thirty. I went to the church to clean up a little, then went to the diner to eat. It was just after dusk when I passed back by the church to get my jacket. The light was fadin', but there he was again. Norman was too busy sweepin' the ground to vandalize anything, but I still wanted to know what he was up to.

He had his back to me and was talkin' to himself as I walked up to him. "Norman," I said, and he jumped another ten feet.

"Don't you have a life, Crenshaw?" He seemed irritated at bein' interrupted.

"I might ask you the same thing, Norman," I countered. "What brings you here this time of day?"

"A little research, Crenshaw." He slid an earpiece back. "Just a little genealogical research."

"You can't hardly see to read the stones," I said.

"Don't need to," he says. "And don't need to be seen, either. People like you ask too many questions. Our friend the constable is another." He took the headphones off and started to pack up.

I pointed to his contraption. "Does the army know you've got that thing?"

"Ever hear of Army surplus, Crenshaw?" He looked me up and down.

"You can't go disturbin' the dead," I cautioned. "Your family might be powerful, but the rest of the town won't take to you botherin' these graves," I warned.

"Don't get your panties in a bunch, Crenshaw. I'm doing this specifically to avoid your concerns." His voice took on that superior Updike air. "Yes, this is your regulation army mine detector— a metal detector, to be exact. I've made some critical modifications for sensitivity." Norman turned to go. "I don't want to be out this late, anyway." He looked 'round like there might be somebody watchin' us. "Nighty- night, Crenshaw," he called over his shoulder as he disappeared into the dark.

~ ~ ~

I didn't mark graves for the three Garrets, not yet. Good thing, too. Vera was first in line and Leyton's coroner was huntin' moose in Canada. Talk was he was pretty steamed at bein' called back. Nearly resigned, they say. Then the tragedy happened to the Garretts, and he had no choice. Took his sweet time, though. Vera's grave went unfilled for a couple of days. That always gives me fits, worryin' that some poor soul might fall in. I lay boards across the openin', but with those vandals 'round....

Reverend Boucher gave a nice service. They say he could have been bishop, but didn't like paperwork. Lydia Updike snagged him for Hollis, one of the few good things she ever did. The Reverend was gettin' on in age. Every year, the rumor went 'round he was to retire after Easter. I think Mrs. Boucher quashed those. She had no desire to have the Reverend under foot.

"Looks like we made it by the skin of our teeth, Weldon," he says to me after the service. Vera's sister and a couple of nephews were among the few who attended. They made their way to a rusting Studebaker and drove off.

"Better get Vera covered up before she floats away."
Reverend Boucher nodded his head to the side. A massive
thunderhead loomed over his shoulder. He headed to the
church with an anxious glance towards the sky.

"Tommy!" I called. "Let's get a move on. There's a bad
sou'wester comin' in." He and I pulled the strips of artificial
grass away from the grave, then the large piece coverin' the
fresh mound of earth that would go back in.

Deke Barbour and his assistant had taken the lowerin'
mechanism and loaded it into the hearse. The assistant was
Deke's oldest boy, Raymond. Good-looking kid, he was
attendin' the local mortuary college in Leyton. I guess they let
him out for special occasions like this. Deke and his boy
didn't talk much. They spoke mostly with looks and gestures.
I suppose it's part of that business.

They were pullin' the canvas awning apart as the winds began
pick up. The undertaker and his son didn't bother foldin' it.
They just shoved it and its frame into the hearse as well. Deke
and his "assistant" ran back for the artificial turf as Tommy
and I shoveled as fast as we could. I could hear a distant clap
of thunder as Deke and his boy drove off.

The rain drops began to hurt as we closed Vera's grave with
the last spadefuls of dirt. I grabbed the shovels and ran for
the church as Tommy sprinted for his car, a 1943 Willy's Jeep
his uncle got from Army surplus.

Lucky I'd left the basement door unlocked, because there was
a huge crack of lightnin' just as I reached it. Drenched, I
leaned the shovels next to the door, my heart poundin'. I
hadn't run like that in ages. Then I realized in all the hubbub

I hadn't paid Tommy. He'd come by tomorrow for it, things bein' tight and all. As the storm pounded outside, I sat down at my desk to do the paperwork the church and village required.

I had just finished with the grave registry when I heard footsteps in the sanctuary overhead. Thinkin' Reverend Boucher was preparin' for next Sunday while waitin' out the storm, I went up to ask about diggin' graves for the three Garretts. They were only occasional churchgoers, and hadn't bought any plots. I reached the top of the stairs and swung the door to the sanctuary open.

"Got a minute, Reverend?" I stopped. The church was empty. I could have sworn I heard someone up here. A panel of one of the stained glass windows was open, lettin' rain blow in on one of the pews. I rushed over to close it. It was the window titled, "And Jesus Wept," showin' Christ standin' at the tomb of Lazarus. Turnin' 'round to inspect the damage, I saw the pew where Lydia Updike used to sit splattered with rain. Splattered everywhere, except where someone had just been sittin'.

I went to the main door and confirmed it was locked. There was no sign of footsteps. The aisles were perfectly dry. Confused, I went back downstairs to get some rags to mop up the water. I had just gotten a towel from the janitor's closet, when someone started down the stairs.

"Who's there?" I called enterin' the stairwell, but there was no one. I felt somethin' brush my ear. Turnin' to see what it was, I was met by nothing, but smelled something from long ago. Despite the rain, I decided I'd had enough exposure to All-

Saints Episcopal for one day. I gathered my things and jogged for home.

~ ~ ~

The next mornin', I didn't need to look for Norman Updike. He came lookin' for me.

"Can't you keep these vandals at bay?" He waved his mine detector at me.

"What did they do now?" I followed him out of the church and out to the graveyard. I stopped as we got to the Updike mausoleum. "How did that happen?"

"How should I know?" Gingerly, Norman pushed the unlocked door aside as if something might spring out. He waited for me to go in first.

A high window on the back wall provided the only light. An aisle roughly the width of a casket separated two walls of niches. Chiseled marble tablets sealed the chambers where Lydia, Avery, and old man Updike rested. I eased my way in. There seemed to be nothing amiss. Three marble panels stood against the back wall, waitin' for the three open niches to be filled. "No damage done," I says.

"I'll be the judge of that," and suddenly, Norman found his spine again. He came in just far enough to satisfy himself that nothing was wrong. He bent to study the door lock. "Doesn't seem forced." He straightened with an odd look on his face, like he was lost in thought. "I want Constable Dodd to take fingerprints. Somebody did this, and I'm gonna find out who."

167

"You'll want to call him then," I said. "As this is your mausoleum, you need to file the complaint."

Norman scowled at me and stepped out to retrieve his mine sweepin' paraphernalia. "I want this locked," he says to me.

"Don't you have a key?" I says, movin' to the door.

"Can't find it," he answers.

Norman, the church, and Deke Barbour were the only ones with keys. I'd almost gotten to the door when something on the floor caught my eye. "What's this?" I reached down for it. "Holy Jesus!" Lydia's diamond engagement ring lay on the floor. I knew it was hers because the last time I saw it, it was on her hand. And she was in her casket, lyin' in state at the church. The other reason I knew it was hers was not too many women in Hollis Depot had six carat diamond rings.

"Give me that!" Norman snatched it out of my hand. He looked more frightened than angry. He stared at it, as if he couldn't figure out how it got there.

"Wasn't that buried with her?" I asked.

"Are you crazy?" Norman sneered. "What would a dead woman need with a ring?"

"It was her last wish," I reminded him.

"Yeah? Well, if wishes were horses we'd be up to our asses in manure." Distracted, Norman slipped the ring into his pocket.

168

I shrugged, steppin' out into the sunlight.

"Leave everything as it is." He picked up his mine detector. "I want Constable Dodd to investigate." He marched off toward the Updike mansion.

I was surprised when Ed Dodd knocked at the door of the boiler room about twenty minutes later. "You open for business?" He leaned his head in.

"I guess so." I stood up and shook his hand. "That was pretty quick." We made our way out and to the mausoleum.

"There may be only one Updike left, but he's just as bad as the rest." Ed Dodd shook his head.

I didn't have to ask. I was sure the threat was real and sincere. "I left everything as we found it," I said as we got to the tomb.

"Good." Ed pulled a jar out of his pocket and a short bristle brush. Unscrewin' the jar, he used the brush to spread a fine powder around the lock.

"Maybe we should call J. Edgar Hoover," I suggested.

"If I thought it would get Norman Updike off my back, I'd call President Truman." Ed frowned as he studied the door. "Nothing. Not squat." He straightened, pausin' to peer into the crypt. "You bring the key?"

"Yup."

"Let me see it." I handed an oversized brass key to the Constable, who studied it. "It's not a common key."

"Nope," I agreed. "I guess they don't want the local locksmith or hardware store cuttin' a duplicate."

"Well," Dodd rose, "No harm done, I suppose."

"Did he find his key?" I asked.

"Not so far," Ed shook his head, examining the deadbolt which was retracted into the lockset. He examined the rear of the door. "No keyhole on this side." He frowned. "Nothing is likely to happen by accident."

"Would you want to be locked inside?" I grinned.

"Depends on whether I'm dead or not." Constable Dodd stepped out of the tomb. "Lock it up." He hooked his thumbs in his belt, a puzzled look on his face.

I pushed the door to and threw the bolt.

"Mind if I borrow that key?" The Constable asked. "I want to see if it showed up at the Dewey's hardware. I also want to make sure Deke Barbour's copy is with him.

"Sure," I shrugged, handin' the key over. I watched Ed Dodd slide it into his shirt pocket, buttonin' the flap shut. "By the way," I asked, "what did old Norman have to say about the ring?"

"Ring?" The Constable stared at me.

"Lydia's ring." I pointed to the mausoleum. "I found it on the floor near the door."

Constable Dodd's eyebrows arched with a look of surprise. "I thought it was buried with her."

"Apparently, Norman had other ideas. But how it got-"

"That S.O.B.!" The Constable bit his lip. "He never said a word. We'll see about that." With that, Constable Dodd marched off, mutterin' about all the other investigations he had to run.

~ ~ ~

The three Garrets went over by the creek. I felt bad, but they were practically charity cases. There weren't any family nearby to handle the arrangements. Eileen's sister came. I guess Clancy's people were out in Oklahoma and unable to make the trip. Deke Barbour spoke with the church board. That's when their financial situation came to light. What little they had went up in smoke with the fire.

To save on expenses, the baby would be in the same casket as Eileen. Still, Deke would have to borrow a second hearse and lowerin' mechanism from the funeral home in Leyton. It was a lot of extra work for a charity case.

"Let's keep it four feet," I said to Tommy, feelin' like I was cheatin' them out of something.

"What'samatter," he grins, "diggin' two holes too much for you?" It was clear he was happy to have the extra work this month.

"Nah," I says, glancin' at the river, "The water table's kinda high here. I wouldn't want them floatin' off."

"Have it your way," he shrugs. "It's twenty bucks a grave either way." Tommy went back to whistlin'. He was always pretty chipper for a grave digger.

We dug 'til nearly noon. I paid Tommy and headed to the church to call Deke to let him know the graves were ready. I couldn't help but pass by the Updike mausoleum. After yesterday and the goin's on, I figured I'd better be vigilant. I don't need any Updikes after my hide. As I approached, I could see the door was shut- one small relief, but there was something layin' on the side. I walked over and was a little surprised. I guess I shouldn't have been. There was old Norman's mine detector lyin' on the ground.

I shook my head and picked it up. Some people can be pretty careless with expensive equipment. That's rich folk for you. It was a pretty heavy thing. I carried it down to my office and leaned it against the wall by the shovels.

I called Deke and let him know he could bring his equipment over, then I turned my attention to old Norman. The phone must've rang a dozen times before he picked up. "Who's there?" He shouted, like there might've been a pink elephant at the other end of the line. There was an edge to his voice and a slur, like he'd been drinkin'.

"Norman? You all right?" I asked, holdin' the phone away from my ear.

"It was damn stupid!" He whispers, like someone was listenin'.

"Listen, Norman, you left your-"

"Destroy it!" He shouts. "Smash it! I don't ever want to see it again."

"I hate to do that, Norman." I says. "It looks pretty expensive."

"It was a mistake." He whispers. "I made it amplify things so I could listen. I thought I could find out about my mother." He trailed off and I could hear his breathin'. It sounded heavy — labored. "It amplified things I hadn't dreamed of…."

"Listen," I says, "why don't I drop it by after-"

"Smash the damned thing!" He screams. "For the love of God, destroy it! Jesus."

I thought I heard him weepin'. Drink affects different people different ways, I suppose. "Listen, Norman," I says kinda quiet, "You'll come back in a couple of days, maybe."

"I can't come back," he weeps. "I stirred things up. I can't stay here. Lydia's mad. She knows what I did."

"Ayup." I says. "Well, I'd better let you go then. You take care, Norman." I hung up, rollin' my eyes. *Pity*, I thought. *He's turnin' out just like his old man.* I shook my head, glancin' at his machine. I didn't know what to do with it. Maybe it was good for locatin' coins and such? I'd give it some thought.

Deke came by, so I had to help him set things up. His "assistant" had exams that mornin'. Can't imagine what that would be like at a mortuary college. Didn't even want to think about what the homework might be.

173

I'll tell you, things get pretty tight with two graves side by side like that, but we managed. Deke wasn't too talkative. This must've been a money-loser for him. He wasn't even usin' the cheap burial vaults, just grave liners. He spread the awning over both holes. That meant the mourners were going to get sunburned, if it didn't rain first. I knew to ask Tommy Detmer along. This would be a hard one.

I meant to say something about Norman to Reverend Boucher next day, but things were too hectic. We had only one set of pallbearers and the space between the graves made maneuverin' difficult. The turnout was more than I would've liked, given the circumstances. There was her sister, his parents and another sibling, plus a few folks Clancy must've worked with at the A&P.

Reverend Boucher did his usual fine job. There wasn't a dry eye in the house. I even thought I saw Deke's son start to tear up. He'll have to watch that if he wants to be any good as a mortician. The mourners filed out, and we got to finishin' things. I'll say one thing, shallow graves make short work. Works better, too, when you aren't racin' a thunderstorm. Still, it was after quittin' time when we closed things up and I made one last stop before heading for home.

The evening sun cast long shadows against the headstones as it set, making the spot seem even more desolate than it normally was. I had seen too many burials to be affected, I thought, but the Garret's funeral bothered me somehow. Another family cut short, I suppose. I stood there, starin' at the cold slab of stone. "I miss you," I said, knowing my wife Emily would never again answer.

~ ~ ~

I came in the next mornin' and set down at my desk. It wasn't 'til I looked up at the calendar from Ferguson's Hardware that it dawned on me what day it was. The week had been so busy, I hadn't realized today was the 30th of October, Devil's night. Given the problems of the past week, I figured I'd better stay 'til midnight to keep the spooks away. Things was pretty quiet except for a hoot owl and some kind of raccoon or opossum rustlin' 'round. I gave up about eleven-thirty and headed home.

Didn't get in until late the next mornin'. That's the best part of the job, bein' your own boss, well practically anyway. Only time the trustees get involved is when the thermostat is too high or low for their comfort, and that's just Sundays.

I was late doin' the paperwork on the Garrets, so that was the first chore of the mornin'. I'd just gotten things wrapped up and was about to check on our coal delivery, when Ed Dodd showed up.

"Pretty gloomy down here," he said glancin' 'round the boiler room.

"Keeps me warm in the winter," I says, "and out of the snow for the most part. What brings you here, Constable?"

"Got your key here somewhere." He began feelin' his pockets. "Seen Norman lately? We've been playing hide and seek."

"Hadn't seen him, but talked to him the other day," I offered. "Wasn't very lucid."

"No?"

"Eleven-o-clock in the mornin' and he was followin' in his father's footsteps."

"Too bad," Constable Dodd nodded knowingly. "Hah!" He reached into his shirt pocket. "The Updike mausoleum key. Ferguson's couldn't duplicate it. Didn't have any blanks that fit and didn't know where to get any either."

I took it and started to hang it on the key board.

"That's a lot of keys there, Weldon."

"Ayup," I agreed.

"You sure that's for the mausoleum?"

"You saw me lock it, didn't you?"

Ed frowned. "Well..."

"Fine." I pulled the key off the hook. "I got nothin' better to do this mornin' anyway." I grabbed my jacket.

There was a frost on the ground when I came in, and it was still there as we headed to the mausoleum, the grass 'round it white and pristine. I was surprised at the cold. This was going to make for a tough Halloween for the kids.

"Jesus H.," I says as we come 'round to the door. It was open again. "Norman's gonna kill me."

"Not likely, Weldon." Dodd stepped forward and pushed the door aside.

"Christ!" I took a swallow of frosty air as I looked in. Poor old Norman. He lay on the floor, his head against the wall. He must've bumped one of the unused marble panels and it had fallen over and crushed him. His eyes, though dead, were open wide with a look of horror on his face.

"So what exactly did Norman say the last time you talked to him?" Ed stepped in.

"Crazy stuff. Said he'd stirred things up. Said Lydia was mad-" I stopped when I saw the other wall. There was a crowbar in the corner, and worse, the marble panel that had covered Lydia's niche lay on the floor.

"I think we'd better call Deke Barbour to clean things up in here." Ed Dodd turned to the open niche. "And that in particular." He stared, pointin' to Lydia's casket.

That Lydia's coffin was open shouldn't have been a surprise. That her shriveled, bony hand protruded from it was a different matter. But it was the fact that her thumb and index finger held the diamond engagement ring — the ring that Norman must have been tryin' to return — that neither Ed nor I will ever be able to explain or forget.

True to his profession, Deke Barbour discreetly moved Norman to the funeral home and prepared him for an appropriately expensive entombment. It was reported that Norman Updike died after a fall in his home. It just happened to be his home for eternity. On a cold day in early November, the last of the Updikes was laid to rest on the spot where he died, not unlike the first Updike in Hollis Depot. Lydia held on to her ring, by the way. After what happened to Norman, no one was about to tempt fate.

Besides Deke, his son, Tommy, and myself; Ed Dodd and Reverend Boucher completed the funeral party. The Reverend spoke briefly and led a prayer. I suspect he scaled back the service to accommodate his limited audience. Tommy and I helped Deke and son seal Norman into his crypt. I turned the lock on the door and removed the key, headin' back to the church with the rest of the mourners.

"What did you do with the extra key?" Ed asked Deke.

"What key?" Deke turned, puzzled.

"Didn't Norman have a key to the mausoleum on him?"

Deke stopped, frownin'. "Come to think of it, no."

"Must've had a key on him," I suggested. "How else could he have gotten in?"

"I went through his pockets," Deke confirmed. "Maybe he dropped it somewhere outside."

"We'll have to look for it," I says. "Can't have folks lettin' themselves in."

"Amen!" The Reverend added.

"Let me know what you find," Ed said as he strode toward his patrol car.

I bade Deke and the Reverend farewell and went back to my office. The boiler room was toasty warm, the one benefit of workin' by the furnace. I didn't want to spend a lot of time lookin' for a key. I'd have to do it soon, before the first snowfall.

I was halfway out of my coat when I stopped, starin' at the wall. The answer lay before me. I moved over to it for a better look. Norman's mine detector had a disk the size of a pie pan at the end of a five foot pole, a wire coiled around it, runnin' into a green canvas shoulder bag that held some kind of electronic gizmo and a heavy dry-cell battery. Another wire ran out of the box to a pair of headphones. I picked the thing up and started for the mausoleum.

The morning sun was finally meltin' the frost in those places where it could sneak past trees and tombstones. You could still see the tracks where we carried Norman's coffin from the hearse to the crypt. I stopped in front of the mausoleum a few feet from the door. If there was a key on the ground, the grass was hidin' it. I hefted the bag onto my shoulder and put the headset on. Funny thing. It had a mouthpiece with a microphone at the end of it. I suppose Norman must've cobbled it together from some other Army surplus he found.

On the face of the electrical box, there was a large toggle switch below some kind of meter along with a knob I assumed would control volume. I flipped the toggle. There was a crack in the earpieces and the needle jumped to the end of the scale before settlin' back to zero. The earpieces were made of black Bakelite and not very comfortable. I moved the disk towards the door. There was no noise in the earpieces at all. The needle stayed at zero. Disappointed, I began arcing out from the door in larger and larger sweeps. Still nothing.

Maybe he busted it when he dropped it, I thought. There was a brass marker a few feet away. I walked over to it to make sure. I lay the disk right on the plaque. Nothing. Zero. I stepped back, disappointed, lettin' the disk set on the ground. "Well, that's a waste of time?" I muttered.

"Hello?" A voice crackled through the headset. It was faint. At first, I thought I'd picked up a radio show.

"Some metal detector you are!" I said to myself. "Can't even get a decent radio show."

"Weldon?" The voice was much stronger. The needle on the dial was slowly climbin'. "Is that you?"

"Hello," I answered. The voice was a woman's. I swore I could recognize it. "Who is this?"

"Why, Helen Lawton, Dear."

I knew that name. How did I know that name?

"Did you get your Psalm memorized, Sweetie?" The chipper voice addressed me as if I were a child.

Psalm? What Psalm? "Where are you, Ms. Lawton?" I began to look 'round for her.

"Down here, silly boy!" The voice was much louder, livlier.

I looked down. The needle on the meter was at the halfway mark.

"Why don't I come up?" The voice said. "I miss a good conversation."

I looked down again, confused, until I glanced at the bronze marker. "NO!" I shouted, turnin' and runnin'. I struggled to take off the headset and shoulder bag as I stumbled. Droppin' them on the ground, I ran to hide in my office. I slammed the door shut and fell against the wall heavin . I must've waited nearly an hour before I could sit at my desk.

He wandered 'round the graveyard, chatterin' to himself. He said it amplified things, things it shouldn't have. That wasn't the half of it! What had Norman done? What had he invented? The bronze plaque said it all. Helen Lawton, my first grade Sunday school teacher, died in the flu epidemic of 1918! What was I to do with that thing lyin' in the middle of the cemetery?

~ ~ ~

Thanksgiving was a week off. We were on our second snow and the air had a cold crispness. These days, I was glad to come to the church — to my office in the boiler room. I leaned back, studyin' the list of maintenance items and drainin' the last of my coffee when I felt a cool touch and a strong scent. Lilacs. Though the spring bloom had long passed, I could smell them, practically touch them. She was back.

"I miss you, Honey." I said without turnin'. There was a light touch on my shoulder. "What's that?" I asked. "You're so faint." I waited. "Yes, you're right," I said. "It's about that time." I rose to get my jacket and Norman's "amplifier." I opened the door and walked toward my wife's grave. "Be right there, Emily," I answered.

Van

Helsing's Curse

"This will be an ugly business, Jonathan. Dangerous, too." Frail but determined, the aging vampire hunter clutched the black leather bag and GPS device as he threaded his way through the crumbling stones in the graveyard. "If you wish to turn back, no one would fault you." His Dutch accent was as thick as the morning fog.

"After what he did to my Lucy?" Despite his determination, there was a nervous catch to Jonathan Harker's voice. He

183

fingered the gold crucifix that hung around his neck. With his other hand, he carried a mallet and a stake of blackthorn. "Will this work, Dr. Van Helsing?"

"Of course, my boy. I have dedicated my life to the pursuit and destruction of the undead." Van Helsing hobbled toward his quarry. "And now, we are on the verge of destroying the root of this evil: Vlad Dracula himself!" He turned to Jonathan and gestured. "We must proceed carefully. Once the sun is up, he will be helpless. But until then, he is qmost formidable. His senses are acute and his powers ungodly."

Reaching an old stone chapel, the pair crept to the wooden bulkhead leading to the basement below. A large padlock and hasp barred their way. "We cannot change into mist and pass through crevasses as he can," the doctor winked at his young friend, "but we do have this." The vampire hunter produced a lock pick and began working on the padlock in earnest. "Lucky, my studies extended beyond the university."

"Doctor," Jonathan whispered, "how can we be sure Dracula is here?"

"We can't, but this is the type of place he would stay. And we have ruined all the remaining hiding places but this."

"Sanctified them, you mean?"

"Precisely!" The vampire hunter grinned. "Thanks to our friend Renfield, poor soul! All of Dracula's sanctuaries are known and purified with garlic and Holy Water." He tinkered with the lock, listening for a response. "My greatest fear is falling under the spell of that undead fiend."

"I don't blame you." Jonathan Harker put a hand to his throat and grimaced at the idea. "Every time I think of poor Lucy-" he stopped short.

There was a faint click and the lock popped open. "There!" Van Helsing uttered with no small satisfaction. He lit an LED flashlight and pushed the bulkhead open, gesturing for Jonathan to follow. "We must be as quiet as possible," he said, descending the stairs into the dank basement. "He will have fed, making him lethargic, which is to our advantage."

He stopped at the foot of the stairs, waiting for Jonathan to lower the bulkhead door and follow. The dirt floor, more than a century old, felt as hard as concrete. The air, heavy with a cold mustiness, seemed to grab at their clothes. The vampire hunter spoke in an urgent whisper, "Remember what you must do, Jonathan. I will locate the coffin. As soon as I raise the lid, You must plant the stake of blackthorn over his heart, take the mallet and strike it with all your might."

"Yes, Doctor." Jonathan's voice cracked.

The aging vampire hunter swung the tiny beam around the room. Many pillars and alcoves revealed a structure built with ancient methods and materials. Cobwebs decorated the corners with the discarded shells of insect victims scattered below. "Ah!" The beam of the tiny flashlight found an oblong box almost in the center of the room. It rested on a pair of well-used sawhorses. "Come," creeping toward it, the vampire hunter whispered to Jonathan.

Van Helsing stood within a foot of the coffin. He looked to confirm his trembling assistant was close at hand. Waiting to make sure Jonathan had his stake and mallet poised to strike, the vampire hunter turned to the casket and its occupant. With a last glance at Jonathan, Van Helsing sprung like someone decades younger and threw the lid open. Before Jonathan could move, a brilliant light blinded them, making them wince.

"There, Senator," a voice from the corner said, "it's just as I said."

"If I hadn't seen it with my own eyes, I wouldn't have believed it." Another man in a three-piece suit stepped toward the pair and into the lights of the camera crew. Accustomed to the camera, he struck a dramatic pose. "And just what do you two think you are doing?" He had the accusatory air of a former prosecutor.

"Senator?" Van Helsing was stunned. He squinted, his eyes adjusting to the bright light.

"Senator William Frost," the man confirmed, making sure his good side faced the camera. "And this is Reverend Alton Wiltshire of the Life League."

"How did you find out about this?" The professor sputtered. "What do you think you are doing?"

"My office received an anonymous tip from a man with a Romanian accent," the Senator sneered. "And we're here to prevent a dastardly crime."

"Crime?" The old man was incredulous. "We have come to destroy the undead!"

"Did you hear that, Senator?" The Reverend, a short, chubby man with a raspy voice, stepped into the camera shot, stroking one of his double chins. "Undead!"

"Undead?" The Senator paused, confused.

"Undead. Unborn. It's all the same," the Reverend insisted. "You heard his admission."

"Indeed I did, Reverend." The Senator held the lapels of his coat and rocked back and forth, sizing up the professor. "That's a confession if ever I heard one."

"Confession?" Van Helsing stepped back confused. "We are here to destroy a vampire, one of the living dead."

"Precisely!" Wiltshire waved a chubby finger in the vampire hunter's face. "The Life League will not stand idly by and let you extinguish the life (or non-life) of this non-dead person."

"But we must release his tormented soul," Van Helsing argued.

"I may profess a faith in the life everlasting, Professor, but that doesn't mean I or anyone else should be in any rush to get there." Wiltshire straightened. "I've instructed my doctors to take whatever heroic measures necessary to prevent an early reunion with my Maker."

"You don't mean to tell me you consider this person living?" Van Helsing stared, aghast.

"Well, he's not rotting," the Reverend replied, noting the well-preserved count bore a striking resemblance to George Hamilton, "and that's good enough for us!"

"And what does that make Vladimir Lenin, then?" Van Helsing stiffened with growing anger.

"A communist!" Senator Frost grinned.

"This man has been dead for centuries!" Van Helsing insisted.

"Well, I played a doctor on television once," the Senator answered, "I know all those terms. And I was up for Bella Lugosi's role in a remake of *Plan Nine from Outer Space*. Undead means not dead. And this man looks pretty undead to me. I won't allow you to tamper with God's plan. We're prepared to hold a prayer vigil here if we have to."

Van Helsing glanced down, sure he saw the vampire smiling.

"Show them the mirror, Doctor," Jonathan interjected.

"Doctor? What kind of doctor?" The Senator demanded.

"One of those pointy-headed university liberals, I'll bet," Reverend Wiltshire started foaming at the mouth. "Probably performs experiments on human blastocysts in his spare time."

The Senator drew a sharp breath. "Potential-baby killer!"

"One moment!" Van Helsing produced a small shaving mirror from the pocket of his jacket. The camera crew shifted for a better shot.

"That's not a valid test for death," the Senator objected. "Why, we don't even accept EEG's or MRI's as proof."

"This isn't for that!" Van Helsing held the mirror angled over the vampire. The image showed an empty coffin. "He casts no reflection because he has no scul."

"Why, if we used that test," the Senator observed, "easily half of Congress would fail."

"Please, Senator, we must destroy this demon before he spreads his evil."

"Write that down, Tommy." The Senator turned to a nearby aide, "The President can use that in his next defense of the death penalty."

Suddenly, the bulkhead door flew open. A network technician with a clipboard stepped in. "Good news, Senator, New York wants a live feed-"

The technician's momentary elation was stilled by a shriek from within the coffin. A beam of the sunlight passing through the bulkhead door struck the vampire's face and disintegrated it and the rest of the count into a foul-smelling cloud. The camera crew doused their light and pointed their camera toward the ground, staring at each other.

"Great," the Senator threw his arms up in disgust, "now what are we supposed to do?"

"Senator," a young aide stepped forward, "there've been reports of zombies in Pascataway, New Jersey."

"Hear that, Reverend?" the Senator perked up. "If we hurry we can still make the six-o-clock news! I'll have to postpone my speech before the disabled American veterans in defense of the war, but what the hey? Great idea, Tommy." He patted the young man on the butt.

There was a mad dash for the stairs as the Senator, Reverend, aides and camera crew bolted out, leaving Van Helsing and Jonathan alone in the dank room.

Jonathan stared at the stake and mallet in his hands. "I guess we won't be needing these," he observed.

"Nonsense, my boy." Van Helsing glanced at the bulkhead with a determined expression. "We need them more than ever. Primary elections are next month."

A Piece of

Cake

"Ain't she a beaut, Willy?" Lyman Woods gripped the steering wheel of the '94 Buick. "Easy pickin's." He gazed at their target, an imposing Victorian house that stood alone in the center of a city block. "Just like the book in the prison library said."

"How old was this book?" Frowning, Willy Steadman stared out through the dark. "Looks like a freakin' war zone," he muttered. Abandoned homes dotted the blocks around the mansion. Many were burned out shells surrounded by vacant lots. All were dark, except for a small light shining in a second story window in their target. "I dunno, Lyme. Don't look very promising to me." He started to pick his nose, but the leather gloves on his hands made that impossible. He blew it on his sleeve instead.

"A piece of cake." Lyman slid the heavy cylinder-puller under his seat. Freed of its lock, the car's ignition switch turned easily. The engine went dead. "Well, let's get going." From the back seat, he grabbed a small black satchel that held tools and sacks and pushed the creaking door open.

"I ain't that sure, Lyme." The smaller man shook his head. "This is pretty risky."

"We'll be done like that." Lyman snapped his fingers, but the glove muffled the sound. "I'll have you reporting to your parole officer before you can say, 'petty thief.'"

Willy remained unmoved. "Awful lot of risk when you don't know what's in there."

"Risk?" Lyman's voice began to rise. "Didn't I take a shiv for you? Didn't I give you an alibi for that last riot in the cell block?" He stared at his partner. "You wanna talk risk?" He threw a ski mask at the figure in the passenger seat. "We're goin' in, Buddy-boy. We are in like Flynn."

The "shiv" Lyman took was an emery board, which earned him a band-aid. And the "riot" was a shove in the line for the prison barber. Willie would have provided Lyman with clarification, if not for the size and attitude of his companion. All of Lyman's stories grew with each retelling.

192

Lyman climbed out of the Buick. He'd parked it a block away under a burned out street lamp. The burly con waited as Willy eased out on his side. "C'mon," he urged the reluctant thief, "we don't got all night."

"Don't they ever change these lights?" Willy stared up at the gloom.

"That's the beauty of it," Lyman said, grinning. "Nobody comes here, not the utility people, especially not the cops." He pushed Willy along. The two looked like a couple of ordinary men, strolling along a deserted street in the early A.M. Still, both men looked over their shoulders as if the houses had eyes.

"It's old money. The book said they owned weaving mills and sold uniforms to the Union troops during the Civil War. Kept their first nickel and invested it. The old bag is the only one left. Must be in her eighties. What kind of fight could she put up?" Lyman snorted, his breath misting in the early November air. "Castleman's mother used to deliver their mail. Got to look inside once or twice. There's gotta be silver and jewelry. And cash! After the Depression, they didn't trust banks."

"Yeah, right," Willy muttered, remembering that "Flim-Flam" Castleman had time added to his sentence for perjury. "This place gives me the creeps."

"Cheer up, Buddy-boy," Lyman grinned. "When we're done, you can have your way with her. A little piece of octogenarian ass? How's that for dessert?"

"Cut it out, Lyman. I don't do that."

"You don't, huh?" Lyman snickered.

"No. I don't," Willy insisted.

"Yeah, right," Lyman said under his breath. "You were in for what?"

"I told you, the D. A. was going for a plea bargain."

"Some bargain," Lyman chortled.

They crossed the street. A rusted wrought-iron fence surrounded the property. Weeds and bushes grew wild, and the lawn looked like it hadn't been mowed in months. A gate stood ajar at the front entrance. The two made a quick turn, circling around to the back. There, the gate was off its hinges. They squeezed through the tight opening, breaking off flakes of rust as they went.

Slipping on their ski masks, the two crept up rickety wooden steps to a massive oak door with beveled glass. Willy raised a crowbar to break the pane.

"Hold it." Lyman stayed his hand. He turned the knob and the heavy door swung open on creaking hinges. "What did I tell ya?" Willy could just make out Lyman's grin in the dark, night air. "Piece of cake."

The two slipped into what must have once been a butler's pantry. Cans, jars and bottles lined dusty shelves. The air was thick with the smell of must. A box of cornflakes lay on its side, a corner chewed off spilling cereal and mouse droppings on the shelf.

A couple of steps led them into a large kitchen. Caked with food spills, a 1950 era range stood along one wall. Two others were lined with glass-faced cabinets. Doors stood ajar, and whatever contents the cabinets held were long-gone. A few dishes, pots and pans were all that were left. Most of them lay on the counter, unwashed. The smell of rotting food hung in the air.

"Jeez," Willy exclaimed as Lyman hushed him up. He motioned for Willy to follow as he eased the kitchen door open. Lyman froze at the sound of voices in one of the rooms down the long hallway. It took him a moment to realize it was a television set. He motioned for Willy to stay as he crept forward to see.

Flickering light danced on an open archway by the front door. Lyman slowed and peered in. Grinning, he motioned for Willy to come. Tiptoeing up, Willy looked in to see a white-haired woman asleep in a stiff-backed armchair. A snowy rerun of "The Beverly Hillbillies" played to a dozing audience.

Willie wondered how they would subdue the woman, but Lyman had already scanned the room and pointed Willy to red silk sash cords that held tattered curtains away from dirty windows. Willy took one side as Lyman was already working a knot out of the other. He was tying a bony wrist to the right arm of the chair as Willy approached the left. Lyman nodded for Willy to start tying as he tied her right ankle to the leg. Willy was doing the left ankle when Lyman got a cord from another curtain and began tying the woman's waist to the back.

A snort made Willy jump, as the old woman began to stir. She had that old person smell Willy remembered from visiting his grandmother's nursing home as a child. The old woman was so frail and tiny, he was sure they could have tied her with dental floss. Only later would Willy wonder if his use of slip knots was such a good idea.

"There!" Lyman stepped back, satisfied. His confidence and volume surprised Willy as it did the old woman.

"What's going on here?" She demanded. "What do you two think you're doing?"

"We're having a tea party, and you're the guest of honor," Lyman chortled.

"Don't worry, Granny," Willy reassured her. "We'll just take a few things and be gone before you know it."

"We'll take our sweet time and give this place a real going over," Lyman corrected him.

"You'll do no such thing!" The woman struggled. "I won't stand for it."

"You'll sit for it, then." Lyman smirked, fashioning a gag from a lace doily that graced the couch behind them.

"You don't know who you are dealing with! Why, I can—" The woman struggled as he forced the dusty cloth into her mouth.

"C'mon. Let's get started." He pulled Willy into the hallway. "Can you beat that?" He shook his head. "What an attitude!"

"Go easy on her, wouldja?" Willy whispered.

"Savin' her for dessert?"

"I told ya, I don't do that anymore!" Willy spoke through gritted teeth. "I'm just sorry for her."

"Sorry she hasn't gotten any lately."

"Your mother wasn't sorry," Willy murmured.

"What was that?"

"Nuthin."

"Better be." Lyman waived him off. "I'll take the dining room. You work upstairs." He handed Willy a sack, then disappeared down the darkened hallway.

Willy surveyed the entryway. A wide stairway hugged the wall by the front door. This door, too, was massive with panes of beveled glass. Willy looked up at the ten-foot ceilings. *No wonder the place feels cold. Must be a bear to heat,* he thought, starting for the stairs. The heavy wooden balustrade wobbled as he climbed creaking treads toward the dank hallway above. It reminded him of his old reform school.

The second floor hallway ran the length of the house. The little illumination there was came from a night light shining from a bathroom down the hall and the moonlight that filtered in through curtained bedroom windows. Willy smelled years of dust as the worn carpet beneath his feet muffled groans of decaying wood. He turned and saw a door at the back of the stairwell. *Must go to the attic,* he thought. *Might as well start at the top.* He touched the brass doorknob as if it might be hot.

Satisfied it wouldn't bite, Willy opened the door to find the second set of stairs he anticipated.

The dimness forced Willy to bring out his tiny flashlight. Its beam was weak and narrow, but it let him see the steps. The handrail was almost off the wall, forcing him to climb slowly. Many of the foster homes Willie had passed through were in a similar state of disrepair. The kitchen was also in pretty sorry condition, for that matter. Judging by the musty smell and dust on the treads, Willy guessed it had been decades since anyone had been this way. He reached the top and was surprised to find a small hallway. Stripped of furniture, two small rooms stood at either side with short, sloping ceilings and tiny windows. Willy guessed they must have been servants' quarters.

Further down the narrow hall, another small bedroom furnished with a rotting mattress lay opposite an ancient bathroom. A claw-foot bathtub and pedestal sink stood on a floor of tiny ceramic hexagons. The toilet tank hung high on the wall with a pull chain. Willy wondered if it still worked, wishing he had taken care of business earlier.

The hall ended with a heavy wooden door with another on the wall to its right. Willy opened this side door to find a second set of stairs. Judging by the smell of rotting food, he guessed they led to the kitchen. He closed the door, nauseous from the odor. *Just like Mom used to make,* he winced. With growing reluctance, the thief turned his attention to the other door. Its knob was an irregular hunk of glass instead of the brass the others used. *Must have been replaced at some time,* Willy guessed, not having seen that style in years. It had an old-fashioned lock you could peer through and open with a skeleton key. He turned the knob.

As he eased the door open, its hinges groaned with resistance. A large, round window at the opposite end of the room let blue moonlight in through broken panes to flood the attic in an eerie glow. A floor of rough planks lay below a tall, raftered ceiling. Willy could just make out starlight through holes in the slate shingles above him. Whatever had been stored in this attic room was long gone. A stray coat hanger and sheaf of paper were all that remained, other than an old rocker that stood facing the window.

Willy moved toward the center of the room only to notice an acrid smell. He looked down to see something other than dust covering the old boards. As he stooped to see what it was, a high-pitched noise overhead caught his attention. He shone his flashlight at the peak above him, but couldn't make anything out in the weak light it produced. "Great. Bats," he muttered.

Something creaking nearby drew his attention. Frowning, Willy swung the beam off the rafters to see a rocking chair in front of the window. He caught his breath as he saw the chair begin slowly rocking back and forth. Willy would have passed it off as a trick of the moonlight except the chair picked up pace.

It stopped short as if an unseen person had gotten out of it. Panicked, Willy turned, bumping the attic door shut. He felt something brush his face and in his terror, he dropped the small light as he jiggled the knob on the door. He felt something at his back and would have sworn someone laid a hand on his shoulder just as he got the door open. Rushing to the far end of the hall, Willy heard the attic door creak shut as he bounded down the stairs. Slamming the stairway door shut, he leaned against it, panting. "I didn't see nuthin'," he kept repeating to himself.

It took him a moment or two to collect himself. Noticing the loot bag in his hand, Willy recalled his purpose for being there and made his way to a bedroom at the front of the house. The bed looked slept-in and the dresser used. *Jackpot,* he thought, *granny-land! Surely she'll have jewelry in here somewhere.*

Willy paused to look around the room. A closet door stood ajar in one corner. Two large windows in adjacent walls were covered with decaying curtains. An open door led to a shared bathroom illuminated by a small oval window. Another bedroom of similar size lay beyond. Willy turned his attention to the dresser, a large Victorian affair with a tall mirror. He rifled through drawers, trying to avoid the heavy undergarments and support stockings. Beneath a pair of long white gloves, he found a velvet-covered case. Willy's eyes twinkled at its contents: a couple dozen loose diamonds, rubies and pearls. *This'll make Lyme-man's day,* he gloated.

The thief slipped it in his sack and paused to look out one of the windows. He could make out the Renaissance Center in the distance, its 70-story hotel marking the heart of Detroit. "What a view," he whispered, catching his own reflection in the glass.

Willy would have gone on to rhapsodize more had it not been for what he saw. Reflected above his shoulder, he saw pair of glowing eyes in the far bathroom doorway. Devoid of body, head or face, they floated toward him, eyes fixed, as it were, on his. Willy turned in panic. Though faint, the two eyes peered at him with a look of shock and terror. Willie's own eyes matched the apparition fear for fear, terror for terror.

If the eyes were in one location, apparently the rest of the spirit did not feel constrained to accompany it. A disembodied voice wailed in Willie's ear, "Get out! Get out."

The eyes had reached the near door of the bathroom as Willy jumped over the bed. He felt something tugging at his shirt, trying to pull him back, as he ran screaming down the stairs. Lyman met him in the hallway. He clamped a hand over Willy's mouth and dragged him into the dining room.

"What's yer problem?" he hissed between clenched teeth. "We ain't here to wake what's left of the neighborhood. Do I gotta twist your head off to keep you quiet?"

"There's weird things goin' on here." Willy panted, worried that Lyman was truly a man of his word. "Chairs move, doors close. And these floating eyes reflect-"

"There's weird things goin' on down there, too." Sneering, Lyman pointed at the dark stain on the crotch of Willy's pants.

Willy flushed with embarrassment. "Yeah, but-"

"But, nothin'," Lyman poked Willy's sternum with a hard index finger. "Houses this old creak and groan all the time. Get over it."

"But-"

"Stop foolin' around." The angry look in Lyman's eyes told Willy to shut up in no uncertain terms. "You better have something to show for your water ballet."

"Uh, sure." Willy fumbled around in the bag for the small velvet case. "Wait'll you see these."

Lyman took the small object, sniffing it as if it was a warm turd.

"Go on. Look inside," Willy urged.

Eyeing his partner, Lyman flipped the lid open. He shined his light on its contents. "Now we're talkin'." A cruel smile flashed across Lyman's face as he moved over to a window. He took one of the loose diamonds and drew it against the glass. The stone made a dull sound, but left no mark. "What the..." Lyman put the gem between his teeth and bit down with a crunch. Spitting out the pieces, he cursed, "Dammit! This is nothing but paste! Cheap costume jewelry." He turned on Willy. "You better come up with something better than this!"

"Well you said this was 'a piece of cake,'" the smaller man countered. "What have _you_ got?"

"Goddam silver plate." Lyman held up a tarnished fork and shot a threatening glance toward the living room. "What is it with people these days? I may have to question the old biddy myself." He turned to see Willy staring over his shoulder. "What now?"

"Jeez. Who's that?" Trembling, Willy pointed at a life-size painting on the wall. A woman in a formal gown stared down at him with a haughty gaze from cruel eyes.

"Oh, her," Lyman snorted. "Don't recognize her? That's the old hag in her younger days."

"I'd hate to run into her."

"Well, you already have."

"Looks like she should be burned at the stake."

"Some of them were." Lyman swung his beam to a second life-sized portrait. It showed a mustached man, dressed as a banker or businessman from an earlier period. He had the same cruel eyes as the woman. "Must've been her old man," Lyman conjectured. "He's the one I wouldn't want to run into. A vicious bootlegger, they say." He turned back to Willy, all business. "Where's your flashlight?"

"Uh, I left it upstairs." Willy pointed, not taking his eyes off the portrait. He was sure the eyes were following him.

"Well, get back up there and keep looking. I'll be in the cellar."

"But, Lyme-"

"Don't 'but' me. Get back up there." Lyman's eyes narrowed. "Wouldn't Three-fingers Mitchell like to know who ratted his brother out to the screws. I wouldn't want to be that poor bastard," Lyman grinned.

"All right," Willy waved him off with a sinking feeling. "I'm goin'. I'm goin'."

Willy crept back up the stairs. He could hear Lyman open the cellar door and switch on the light. "Pushy bastard," Willie cursed under his breath as the sound of Lyman's footsteps receded into the basement. Willy took his time climbing the stairs. More than once, he looked back to see if anything was following him. Finally reaching the top, Willy didn't even look back at the two front bedrooms. And there was no way he was going to go to the attic for his flashlight. Instead, he decided it would be safer to plow fresh ground, so to speak, and work the back bedrooms.

The first had a single unmade bed and an empty dresser. The closet was bare, too. Willy presumed it must have been a guest room. Avoiding the mirror, he passed through the shared bath to the next bedroom. From its appointments and the contents of the dresser drawers and closet, Willy could tell this was once a man's room. Double-breasted suits and two-tone shoes from another period filled the closet.

Though it was dark, Willy set out searching the dresser. If he was lucky, he might find gold cufflinks or a pocket watch, but he didn't hold out much hope. He got as far as the bottom drawer when he heard someone climbing the stairs. A strange voice kept saying something Willie couldn't understand and the steps were too confident and energetic to be Lyman's. Panic began to set in as Willy heard whoever it was reach the landing. He searched for a hiding place as the footsteps came down the hall. Desperate, Willy took a calculated risk and slid under the bed.

He could feel his heart pounding as the steps reached the door of the bedroom and grew closer. From his vantage point, Willy saw a cuffed pair of pinstripe trousers and clunky black wingtip shoes topped with white spats. He held his breath, wondering what would happen next when the mattress sagged and groaned above him. Whoever or whatever it was, it was sitting on the bed, directly above his head.

The thief watched the legs fade upward into mist. Had he not done so already, Willy would have wet himself. Suddenly, the mattress sprang to life. Different segments came shooting down as if someone was jumping all over the bed. Rusting springs complained in loud squeaks all around him. Paralyzed with fear, Willy could only wait and see what would happen next. Five or ten minutes must have passed before the bed stopped shaking.

He wanted to scream, but waited to make sure whatever it was had gone. After twenty minutes, and dripping with sweat, Willy started to make his way out from under the bed. His hand brushed something soft. The thief turned to see what it was. Though the light was dim, Willy saw he was staring face-to-mummified-face with a long-dead body. Any remaining possibility of quiet vanished as, screaming, Willy shot out from under the bed.

The fresh, damp spot in his crotch was the last thing on Willy's mind as he hit the bottom stair. He looked frantically for Lyman, then remembered his partner in crime was in the cellar. Not wishing to overstay his welcome, the frightened robber was willing at this point to walk home, Lyman or no Lyman. Willy rushed to the living room to make his farewells to the old woman.

"Lady, there is something very bad going on here..." Willy would have continued, but the old woman wasn't sitting in the chair anymore. The curtain ties lay on the floor. Instead, an eyeless ghoul, white hair billowing from rotting scalp, rose to greet him. Screaming, Willy ran to the entryway followed by his new-found "friend." Cursing and crying, he struggled with the knob to the massive door before finding the release to the latch. Wherever the old lady had gotten to, it was no longer his concern.

~ ~ ~

In the early morning moonlight, a stray dog paused from dining on a dead bucket of fried chicken to watch a man in a black ski mask run screaming by. It did not require the dog's acute smell to tell the man had a load in his pants. Waiting a moment for the air to clear, the dog resumed its extra-crispy meal to the sounds of sobbing and wailing fading in the distance.

~ ~ ~

"GODDAMMIT!" The noise upstairs made Lyman jump and hit his head on a low-lying heating duct. "I'm gonna kill him before I'm done," he muttered, rubbing his head. "Him and that old biddy."

Lyman would have done so then and there, but he was contorted behind a massive coal-burning furnace. Having exhausted all other possibilities in the cellar, he was not leaving this job without something, even if that meant taking the fuses from the fuse box. A cast iron door in the stone wall of the foundation caught his attention. He crawled toward it. At floor level and no more than two feet square, Lyman guessed it led to the coal bin— the room where the coal used to be stored before it was burned.

The iron door was heavy, but still swung freely once Lyman raised its latch. Most doors like this were sealed when these old furnaces were converted to oil or gas. It seemed odd to find this one working. Lyman swung the beam of the tiny light into

206

the blackness. The coal must have left its mark, which didn't help the fact that his battery was giving out. He made a final pass with the light and caught the glint of something shiny and metallic.

Encouraged, Lyman squeezed through the door. It was a tight fit and lumps of coal dug into his knees, but Lyman made it in. Once there, he was able to stand, somewhat. The room was maybe five feet tall. He swung the dimming beam to where he thought he saw the metal. It was near a back wall. Lyman reached down and picked up a tooth with a gold crown.

"What the..." He studied the object in the dimming light. "How did that get in here?" He set out to survey the rest of the room. It appeared to be ten by twelve. An opening in the far wall, probably where the coal chute once was, had been bricked up. He made his way around the perimeter back to the door. He paused his light on the bundle of cloth next to the door. Lyman stopped, realizing he'd crawled over this. Looking closer, he saw the skull and grew concerned he was looking at a skeleton. He played the dimming beam of light around and found clothes containing a second skeleton nearby, black wingtips and white spats on boney feet.

"This can't be good," Lyman muttered as made for the door. The crook started to crouch down just as the iron door clanged shut. He heard the latch drop into place. "Oh, Jesus," he cried and began to pound on the metal with his flashlight. "Can anybody hear me?" He shouted. "Anybody? Willy? You there?" He asked as the flashlight went out. "Willy! Answer me, dammit! Answer me!" he pleaded to the lonely echo of his own voice.

~ ~ ~

"You'll have to forgive me." The old woman withdrew the latch and opened the massive door to the two blue uniformed men standing before it. "I'm not as fast as I used to be." She stepped away from the doorway and the morning light.

"No problem, Ma'am." The older of the two came in first. He stopped to look up at the tall ceiling of the foyer. "We're with the Detroit police, Ma'am. My name is Foley and this is Sergeant Martin." The close-cropped blond nodded, looking around. "And you would be?"

"Lydia Updike." She took his hand and smiled behind cold, gray eyes. "What can I do for you?"

"Well, Ma'am," the older officer continued, "we discovered a stolen car about a block away, and since you're the only person around, we wondered if you had seen or heard anything?"

"Me?" She smiled. "Certainly not. This place is dead. Has been for years. No one comes here anymore. Not a living soul!"

"I'm sure, Ma'am, but still-"

"It's almost lunchtime." She took the officer's hand. "And I never get any visitors. Can I interest you boys in something special? How about a piece of cake?"

ONCE

MORE, WITH FEELING

The face in the mirror seemed strange yet familiar. "Look at that gut!" Avery Loring grimaced at the alien reflection: a forty-ish male with receding hair and an expanding waistline. "Who's gonna want to date an old fart like you?" He frowned, trying to pull his stomach in, but finally gave up. "Am I growing boobs? Jeez!" Sighing, he resumed the last of his shaving, resigned to an intense weightlifting regimen at the gym.

His appearance hadn't mattered until after the divorce. *How insensitive of Emily to run off with her yoga instructor. Bitch!* He shook his head, wondering how to climb out of his funk. *A change in lifestyle, perhaps? Not a chance!*

Since the divorce, his days seemed to take on a deja-vu quality of monotonous repetition. He wondered how often he had, or would continue to repeat this routine. Frowning, he mopped his face with a towel and left the bathroom to dress for work.

~ ~ ~

"How's it going, Sport?"

The electrical engineer felt a hand on his back and looked up from his screen. Avery was at a critical point in designing the logic module for a stabilization circuit and didn't want the interruption; still, it was the boss, who was unusually chummy this morning. "Uh, not bad, Ted. What's up?"

"Up? Nothing really." He scanned Avery's work. "Just touching base." He cocked his head. "How are you doing with your…"

"Image stabilizer? Pretty good." Avery leaned back, putting his hands behind his head. "I'm probably a week ahead." As soon as the words came out, he regretted it.

"Really?" Ted perked up like a bear in a salmon run.

Avery sat straight. "Of course, anything might go wrong."

"Then again, maybe it won't. Just call me a cock-eyed optimist," Ted winked. "Not to change the subject, but how's single life?"

Avery shrugged. "Not bad. Not great."

"Hmm." Ted looked thoughtful. "Haven't replaced the ex-, yet?"

"Working on it. Nobody steady, though."

"No one waiting at home with your slippers and a drink? Hmmm?" Ted almost achieved sincerity. "Well, give it time, Sport."

Avery watched his boss carefully. The wheels were definitely turning. So was Avery's stomach. Ted was younger than Avery — younger than most anyone at the company. Ambitious, he was considered a climber even by the climbers in the Vantech corporation. Avery was happy just to stay out of his sights. Finally, Avery grew concerned by the attention. "Can I do something for you?" Almost immediately, he was sorry he asked that question, too.

"Funny you should ask." Ted stared at him as if he were a cherry on an ice cream sundae. "Are you familiar with the Chronodyne project?"

"No."

"Good." Ted smiled. "You shouldn't be. It's very hush-hush. I don't even know that much about it except they're in a remote building just off-campus." He shifted, moving around Avery, like a tiger stalking prey. "They report directly to the chairman."

Avery's eyebrows raised at the revelation. The boss was looking to score brownie points with the big guy. *Shields up, Mr. Sulu.* "What has this got to do with—"

"Always one step ahead, Avery. That's what I like about you!" Ted grinned, his capped teeth looking perfectly white, making Avery uneasy. "They're looking for someone with your background to help out temporarily."

"Well, I really..." Avery looked at the circuit design.

"It shouldn't take more than a week, and think of the exposure!" Ted's stare was intense. "I insist," he grinned. "You deserve some time in the spotlight."

~ ~ ~

Avery stepped out of his car, rough gravel crunching under his feet. *The boss was right. This place was way out of the way.* He'd had to double back to find the dirt road that ran the mile to this sheet metal building that looked like a Quonset hut. *What could they be doing here?* He wondered.

Given the informality of his surroundings, he eased the single door of the building open, rather than knock. An odd collection of machine tools and scientific equipment greeted him. Several large tanks, covered in frost, lined the wall. Avery thought they could be Dewar flasks containing liquid nitrogen. Insulated piping ran from the tanks over to a geodesic ball some twelve feet in diameter. The outside was covered in wires and electronic devices Avery had never seen before.

212

"Got any idea what it's for?" Avery was startled by the man in the dirty white lab coat. Somehow, it seemed appropriate for the stocky, bearded man wearing it. "You must be Loring." He clapped Avery on the shoulder and shook his hand with enthusiasm.

"Uh, yes," Avery stammered. "They didn't say much at headquarters."

"But you took the survey and signed the release, right?"

"Well, yes," Avery affirmed. "And the nondisclosure agreement, but they didn't even-"

"Ah, yes." The burly man laughed. "Very secretive at HQ, aren't they? I'm Dr. Chesterton. You can call me Keith. We're not very formal here." coat. It was smeared with grease and other fluids Avery couldn't identify.

"We?"

"Yes, Weinstock and myself." He called over his shoulder, "Greg! Come over here and meet..."

"Avery."

"Right! Avery."

A gaunt-looking man with dark disheveled hair crawled out from behind the geodesic ball. "I think I've evened out the distribution. Hi. Nice to meet you." He shook Avery's hand. "Greg Weinstock."

"Avery Loring." He glanced at the dome. "Nitrogen?"

213

"Liquid nitrogen?" Weinstock grinned. "Or were you thinking nitroglycerine?"

"No, not exactly." Avery looked from one man to the other. "They really haven't told me anything."

"Ah." Chesterton nodded. "You're an electrical engineer, aren't you?"

"Yes," Avery nodded.

"Then you know about phase changes. We're getting superconductivity around 39 degrees Kelvin. But we really don't see any tunneling effect until 25."

"Oh, sure," Avery replied, not sure at all.

"With liquid helium, we can get to 4.2 degrees Kelvin!" Weinstock boasted.

"Okay," Avery waited for the punch line.

"Didn't they teach you about the Josephson effect?" Chesterton stared at Avery like he was wearing his underwear on the outside.

"Resistance decreases and current flow increases as you approach absolute zero until current persists without externally applied voltage." Avery nodded. "I see you're working on a super computer using Josephson junctions. You might recall IBM tried that in the 70's."

"Yes," Weinstock grinned. "That's exactly what we want corporate to think."

214

"You realize they also have use in quantum-mechanical applications?" Chesterton asked.

"Sure," Avery agreed. "So?"

"So, IBM killed off their project when it didn't deliver the performance they expected." Weinstock snickered.

"What they didn't realize," Chesterton continued, "was that the Josephson devices were throwing off their measurements because they were also warping time!"

"Huh?" Avery wasn't quite following things.

"At 25 Kelvin, electrons tunnel through insulators." Weinstock passed his right hand through two left fingers.

"Below 10 degrees, they form wormholes!" Chesterton raised an index finger. "Very tiny ones, perhaps, but wormholes nonetheless!"

"That's nice." Avery started backing towards the door.

"Ever heard of Visser's 'Roman ring'?"

Avery shook his head.

"He postulated that if you arranged X-number of wormholes into a tetrahedron or dodecahedron, you could create a time machine."

"You mean-" Avery pointed at the geodesic ball.

"Exactly! He simply lacked the means of generating wormholes."

"We told corporate the processor complexes were arranged that way for maximum throughput," Weinstock giggled.

Avery grew skeptical. "And I suppose it works?"

"As far as we know." Chesterton shrugged.

"Everything we put in comes back unchanged." Weinstock complained.

"We put a digital video camera in and got footage of a night sky with constellations we couldn't identify." Chesterton put his hand on Avery's shoulder. "We're beyond the passive testing stage."

Avery looked around for the exit. "We'll, that's good to know. I really appreciate the tour-"

"But you haven't seen anything," Chesterton objected as Weinstock began to push Avery from behind. "We're quite serious about this!"

"Nobel material, for sure," Weinstock boasted.

"For the two of you." Avery let himself be led further into the lab.

"The three of us," Chesterton threw the offer out as Weinstock glowered. "What were the first words spoken on a telephone?"

Avery paused and thought. "'Watson, come here. I need you.'?"

216

"Exactly!" Chesterton agreed. "Thus giving Watson immortality, historically speaking."

"And Samuel Morse sent 'What hath God wrought?' over the telegraph, but I don't see where He cashed in."

"Fame is relative, Mr. Loring. God was doing just fine before the free plug." Chesterton led him to a large console with dials, valves and buttons. "Got it at a steal." Chesterton patted the top. "Overstock from G.E.'s reactor division." He caught the look of concern on Avery's face. "Just kidding. It's from North Korea."

A pair of computer displays sat flush with the surface of the controls. Some of the wires ran out to control valves on the Dewar flasks. Others led to the geodesic ball where they fanned out over its surface to Frisbee-sized electronics modules. There were insulated tubes running into and out of each module. Wisps of white vapor hissed out from where the tubing attached to the frosty circuitry.

"We try to vent the helium as it gasifies," Chesterton explained. "Still, given the temperature extremes, there's some leakage."

"Looks like the modules are at optimal temperature, Keith."

"Good, good." Chesterton rubbed his hands as if they were cold. "You must have some questions, Loring."

Avery perused the large structure. "Why don't you use animals?"

"We have," Chesterton assured him. "But they can't tell us where they've been or what they've seen. At this point, we need some intelligence."

"So, you use this to send me somewhere in time. How am I supposed to get back?"

"That's the beauty of it, Loring. You never really leave our time. It just extends ours into another. Like being in a bubble underwater."

"As long as the circuits are turned on," Weinstock added.

"Yes, that's right," Chesterton affirmed. "Sort of a built-in safety feature. No power, no travel."

"And just where would I go?" Alexander Graham Bell's historic call to his assistant rang in Avery's ears.

"That's where we need your help." Chesterton held his fingertips together. "I think that firing the circuit pods in different sequences, plus power and duration would affect that."

"Hmmm." An engineering problem. That always intrigued Avery. "You'd ease into this?"

"Of course."

"Short little trips at first?"

"Solid research technique all the way." Chesterton reached into a pocket and held something out to Avery.

"What is this?" Avery picked up a peanut-sized device.

"Bluetooth headset. Put it over your ear."

Avery examined it and then hung the loop behind his ear. "You expect this to work across time?"

"As I said, Avery, we're not sending you through time. We're simply extending our bubble of time into another. You just happen to be standing in the middle of it."

"I don't know..." Avery shook his head.

"Thirty seconds." Chesterton patted Avery's shoulder reassuringly as Weinstock moved to the geodesic ball. "What could it hurt?"

"I really don't..." Avery began to weaken.

"Last year's Nobel prize in physics was $1.5 million."

At that, Weinstock swung a large section of the ball open. In light of his divorce, Avery realized his ex- could never come after his share of the prize. He was torn between greed and revenge. Let's see her aerobics instructor earn that!

He stooped to get into the ball. It was larger than he expected. There was a low platform of metal mesh to stand on. It protected the electronics module underneath. Avery looked around as Weinstock closed the hatch. There were no lights. Plenty of open spaces in the structure made that unnecessary. He studied the equipment surrounding him. It was like being under a metal grape arbor.

"Put it in." Chesterton called from behind the console.

"What?" Avery turned and cupped his ear.

"The Bluetooth headset," Chesterton clarified his instructions. "Press the side button until it activates, then put it in your ear."

Avery held the small device out to study it. About as large as a circus peanut, the headset had an ear loop and a frosted button on the side. He held it in and waited. In a few seconds, the button began to flash. Avery looped it over his ear.

"There are volume buttons on the top." Chesterton's voice came through loud and clear.

"No, I'm fine," Avery assured him. "Am I coming through, okay?"

"Perfect!" There was glee in Chesterton's voice. "We're going to start with baby steps. Thirty seconds on low power. Ready?" Chesterton's voice crackled over the headset.

About to reply, a sudden thought struck Avery. "Why don't you send Weinstock?" He demanded.

"Then who would help run the experiment?"

Chesterton's answer seemed reasonable. "Ready," Avery responded with minimal enthusiasm.

"What's our temp?" Chesterton's voice was clear.

"Twenty-nine and falling," Weinstock sounded matter-of-fact.

"Powering circuits now," Chesterton spoke calmly. "You might be interested to know, Avery, we're giving the computer chess problems. It is, after all, a fully functional super computer."

"It's beaten Deep Blue six times so far," Weinstock boasted. His voice sounded remote. Avery surmised he was standing away from the mike.

There was little noise other than a faint hum and the hiss of escaping gas. For the first time, Avery noticed he was cold, which was not surprising given the freezing apparatus surrounding him. "I'm going to need a sweater," he complained as the geodesic ball dissolved into nothing. "Hey!" Avery shouted.

Chesterton sounded clinical. "What do you see?"

"The machine disappeared."

"Not surprising. It isn't part of the time envelope. It just creates it."

"I'm still in the lab." Avery stared openmouthed as he watched himself enter the building. "Boy, am I out of shape," he blurted out.

"What was that?" Chesterton's voice took on an air of curiosity.

"I'm watching you and Weinstock give me the tour. I gotta work on my gut." Avery would have given a blow-by-blow, but the geodesic ball rematerialized. "Hey! What happened?"

The door swung open and Weinstock stepped back to let Avery out. Weinstock stared at him as if he were a specimen. "Ten fingers? Ten toes?" He asked, making Avery look down at his hands.

"Why would that change?" Avery stared at Weinstock then Chesterton. "What gives? You cut it short, didn't you?"

"It was a good start." Chesterton stated, but didn't look Avery in the eye. "No need to tempt fate further until we study the data."

"Tempt fate?" Avery stepped closer.

"Your encounter with yourself reminded me of several time paradoxes we need to avoid or at least consider."

"Such as?"

"Like killing your grandfather." Weinstock closed the hatch on the globe and joined them.

"Why would I kill my grandfather?"

"It isn't that you would, but that you could." Chesterton spoke as he studied data on the computer screen. "The fact that it is possible suggests that even minor alterations to your ancestry could have devastating effects."

"Kill Dad or Gramps and it's suicide by time travel." Weinstock stopped at Chesterton's icy glare.

"What my assistant is saying so poorly, is that one mistake and you could do away with your own existence."

"Oh," Avery nodded, considering the possibility.

"Any interaction with the past, however minor, could alter the future, or in our case, the present." Chesterton propped his jaw up with his hand, thinking. "Are you familiar with chaos theory? The butterfly effect?"

"The movie?"

"Please tell me you don't do all your scientific research in Hollywood, Mr. Loring." Chesterton shook his head. "It refers to an iterated nonlinear system's sensitivity to trivial changes in a non-adjacent field array. In chaos theory, the butterfly effect suggests that, under the right circumstances, the mere beating of a butterfly's wings in one location on the planet can lead to a hurricane in another."

"Oh." Avery's brow furrowed as he pondered how that would work. "A tiny cause produces an unexpectedly larger effect."

"And don't forget temporal loops!" Ever helpful, Weinstock looked Avery up and down, making notes on a clipboard.

"Yes. Thank you, Weinstock." Chesterton turned to Avery. "Another theory holds that if you disturb time, you can create a situation where the same time sequence loops over and over like a broken record."

"You didn't mention this before."

"I didn't think we'd be so successful." Chesterton stroked his beard. "Still, I suppose..."

"You suppose what?" Avery frowned.

"I suppose if you stay within the 'time bubble' nothing can go wrong."

"That's reassuring." Avery grimaced. "I'm not sure I can handle this."

"Can you handle standing in one spot?" Chesterton stared at him as if he were a recalcitrant child.

"Tell him what MacArthur Genius grants are going for," Weinstock interjected.

"Just tell me what a third of one comes to," Avery shot back.

"All right." Chesterton snapped forward. "We'll get nowhere bickering. It's time to see if we can control the journey."

"How's that?" Avery asked.

"Power and duration determine distance, just like an automobile. Except in this case, our road is time." Chesterton returned to the data on his screen. "There is a threshold at which travel occurs, another where position is maintained. We just marked it. Take power away, and the traveler returns-"

"Like a yo-yo," Avery finished the sentence.

"Not the simile I would have used, but in essence, the concept."

Avery began to think about the money he wouldn't be sharing with his ex-. "When's the next trip?"

224

"In a few minutes, once we reset things."

Chesterton and Weinstock busied themselves at the console as Avery watched. The knobs and valves controlled the liquid helium. Some of the dials registered the tank temperature and pressure. Other gauges monitored each of the electronics modules. By Avery's count, there must have been two dozen of them. The computer screens had windows showing many chess programs in progress, plus controls to increase or decrease the priority the processors gave to the chess program. There were windows, too, that registered the overall condition and performance of the system.

"Does it go forward as well as backward?" Avery leaned over Chesterton's shoulder.

"Funny you should ask." Chesterton didn't bother looking up. "Currently the circuit paths are arranged so that the electrons tunnel towards the center. If my theory is correct, having them tunnel outward would push the bubble forward." He opened a valve and watched the indicators on the individual modules. "Unfortunately, reorienting the circuits would take time. Perhaps in the future, if you'll forgive the pun."

"Dr. Chesterton, module twenty-five dash thirty is drifting off-norm." Weinstock looked over at his boss. "It's sliding hot."

"Adjust it, would you?" Chesterton was preoccupied with a calculation as Weinstock grabbed a small wrench and walked towards the globe. Avery drew in his breath when the project lead pulled out a slide rule. "Come now, Loring. Don't tell me you've never seen one of these before?"

"They told us about them in freshman engineering, but-"

"But what?" Chesterton slid the center bar and glide line to read a result, which he keyed into the computer.

"I thought you'd want something more accurate."

"In the right hands, Mr. Loring, these are just as good as the massive computer complex over there." Chesterton looked up as Weinstock returned.

"Got it." Weinstock plopped into his chair and let the wrench clatter onto the console's countertop.

"What we will do this time," Chesterton turned to his experimental subject, "is drop the temperature a degree and bring more processors online. That should increase the effect. I'm hoping to send you back about a thousand years."

"I see." But Avery was still feeling disconcerted by the presence of Chesterton's slide rule.

"We're at twenty-four and holding," Weinstock announced.

"Good." Chesterton turned to Avery. "Looks like we're ready." He nodded to Weinstock, who led Avery back over to the globe.

Avery stepped through the portal more quickly this time, but with no greater assurance. He grimaced as Weinstock sealed him in. He looked around, wondering if the mere exposure to electromagnetic radiation, not to mention in these quantities, would leave him sterile. His worries were interrupted.

"Sound check," Chesterton squawked unto Avery's earpiece. "You there, Avery?"

"Yeah. Sure." Avery frowned. His stomach was generating its own "butterfly effect."

"'Once more unto the breach, dear friends,'" Chesterton's use of Shakespeare was lost on Avery as the globe dissolved again. It took longer this time, he noted as a new landscape appeared around him.

Avery found himself in the middle of a forest. From the chill in the air and the color of the leaves, he determined it was early fall. He could hear birds chirping and the rustling of squirrels on the forest floor. He noted something else, too: the smell of distant smoke. Somewhere nearby, someone was cooking with a hardwood fire. Avery started to wonder. "Dr. Chesterton, am I supposed to be able to smell things?"

The answer didn't come right away. "Interesting," Chesterton finally responded. "I suppose if you can see things, I don't see why you couldn't smell them as well."

Avery started to ask a follow-up question, but a noise drew his attention to his left. Something much larger than a squirrel was approaching. He watched as the branches of a wild lilac parted. A youth, rather small in stature, peered out, seeking something. He wore only a buckskin loincloth and carried a bow and arrow. Avery assumed he was stalking prey and watched with interest.

The youth spotted something and raised his bow to draw back his arrow. Avery turned to see his target: a large black bear grazing on a blueberry bush. The youth seemed intent on striking his target and might have succeeded if Avery hadn't sneezed at that moment. As the bear turned around, the youth pivoted and stared openmouthed at Avery, who returned the same jaws-agape greeting.

Frightened, the youth spun around to flee and ran straight into a tree, knocking himself out cold. Avery stared at the prone figure as the bear drew closer. Avery wondered if he should deliver some kind of aid or at least distract the bear. He whispered into the headset, "Dr. Chesterton, am I supposed to be visible?" In reply, the geodesic ball rematerialized around him.

~ ~ ~

As the hatch cracked open, Avery pushed it aside and rushed to Dr. Chesterton. "Am I supposed to visible? I think a native of the period saw me."

Thoughtful, Chesterton stroked the smooth skin of his face. "Did you hear that, Weissberg? You were right. I owe you a Coke"

Grinning in victory, the Nordic-featured assistant leaned against the console, running thin fingers through stringy, blonde hair. "It stands to reason things should go both ways."

"Are we sure this is such a good idea?" Avery frowned. "Something doesn't feel right," he said, scratching his chin. "If things like sight and smell can transcend the bubble, who's to say things and people can't cross over, too?"

"He's got a point, Doc," Weissberg agreed.

"I've got a hunger, too." It occurred to Avery his queasy feeling might be due to the fact that lunch had passed hours ago.

228

"Look, just stay within the time bubble, don't take anything and don't leave anything, and you'll be fine," Chesterton reassured him. "I want to try a big jump next — pre-ice age! Weissberg, get him that PB&J from last Thursday, would you?"

Weissberg strode over to a filing cabinet with a combination lock on it. He turned the dial for a minute before pulling the drawer out. He approached Avery with a brown paper bag. "Here. We get involved and forget to eat."

Avery stared at the peanut butter and jelly sandwich as he watched Chesterton and Weissberg set up for the next trip. Avery's beard began to itch. He scratched it absent-mindedly at first, then stroked it, considering possible complications to time travel. In Avery's imagination, butterflies circled his murdered grandfather in an endless loop.

Before he knew it, Avery was being ushered to the time globe. As he climbed in, Weissberg shoved a small digital camcorder into his hands, forcing Avery to stuff the sandwich into his pocket.

"Here," Weissberg commanded. "You know how to use one of these, right? It's already powered on. Remember to take the lens cap off. If you run into a pterodactyl, I want proof."

With those reassuring words, the hatch closed and Avery stood in the center of humming circuitry and hissing coolant. This time the globe seemed to expand before it dissolved. Or am I getting smaller? Avery wondered. As the globe fully dissolved, he found himself standing at the edge of a vast open field of tall grasses. A meadow? He wondered. No, something much larger.

"What do you see, Avery?"

"Not much, Dr. Chesterton. It looks like a prairie."

"Can you identify any plants or animals?"

"Not really." Avery put the video camera viewfinder to his eye and panned the scene. "No, nothing distinctive."

At that, something blocked his view. Avery pushed the camera back from his eye to see a large butterfly perched on the lens. He began to sweat. At first he blew on the insect, trying to dislodge it. When that failed, he tried violently shaking the camera and saying "shoo," but the bug was fixed in the video camera. At last, he tapped the wing with his finger. With intense relief, Avery watched the insect flutter off.

"That was close," he muttered.

"What was?" Came the reply on his headset.

"There was a butterf—"

Something substantial was touching Avery on the shoulder, only it wasn't a hand and it was more like a tentacle feeling him out.

"What's that, Avery? I didn't copy. There was a what?"

But Avery had turned to look. It was eight feet tall and hairy. Two large eyes topped a wide face with a three foot undulating nose. A pair of foot-long tusks framed the mouth.

"A woolly mammoth." Shock and panic had overtaken Avery.

230

"Great! You're pre-ice age. Be sure to tape it."

Almost eye-to-eye with Avery, the mammoth's trunk made a lunge for the peanut butter and jelly sandwich in his pocket. Avery swerved, but lost his balance. Screaming, he fell off the platform, his only link to the time globe, and into the tall grass.

The mammoth was undeterred. It approached Avery as he scrambled to his feet and began backing up. "What do I do now?" He called into the headset, but got nothing back. He guessed once off the platform, he was out of the bubble and the link was broken. "Nice mammoth," he held his hands in a defensive position and kept backing away.

The animal was hungry and determined. It pressed on. "Now, now." Avery cautioned. He was being driven further and further away from the platform. He would lose it in the tall grass and be left behind if he didn't do something. He grabbed the remains of the sandwich and threw them as far as he could to his left.

The animal made a trumpeting sound and started after the sandwich. Avery turned back to where he thought the platform was, but any momentary relief Avery might have felt was dashed by the loud trumpeting sound that came from the edge of the clearing. At twice the size of his peanut butter munching nemesis, the mother mammoth easily parted the trees to enter the grassland. With tusks four feet long, she made a beeline for Avery.

He ran, trying to keep the mammoth calf between himself and the mother, but with six foot strides, she could easily outrun him. Desperate, he knew he had to divert the mother in order to escape. *Temporal doomafligees be damned*, he thought. *I gotta do something fast! I don't want to spend the rest of my life without Monday Night Football.*

The thought proved to be inspirational. Avery cocked his right arm back and with all his might flung the camcorder at the mammoth calf. It hit just behind the left ear, and the calf sank to the ground with a shuddering thud. As the mother prodded the prone baby with her trunk, Avery made a mad dash for the time globe's platform.

"For the love of God, get me outta here!" He screamed on mounting the platform. "Do you hear me?" He pleaded as the mother mammoth came charging. "Get me the fu-"

~ ~ ~

The face in the mirror seemed strange yet familiar. "Look at those boobs!" April Loring grimaced at the alien reflection: a forty-ish female with a descending chest and extending hips. "Who's going to want to date an old tart like you?" She frowned, trying to throw her shoulders back, but finally gave up. "Am I growing a mustache?" Sighing, she resumed applying her mascara, resigned to an intense aerobics regimen at the gym.

Her appearance hadn't mattered until after the divorce. *How insensitive of Earl to run off with that aerobics instructor. Bastard!* She shook her head, wondering how to climb out of her funk. *A change in lifestyle, perhaps? Not a chance!*